CRASH

_____

GRAHAME CLAIRE

Crash (Crash & Burn Duet, Book One) Grahame Claire

Copyright © 2021 Grahame Claire

Editing And Proofreading:

Marion Archer, Marion Making Manuscripts

Karen Lawson and Janet Hitchcock, The Proof is in the Reading

Lori Sabin

Ebook ISBN: 978-1-951878-09-2

For those who crash and dust themselves off.

CHAPTER ONE

PEPPER

"DID your dog just piss on my truck?"

Muffy lowered his—yes, *his*—leg and wagged his tail as he blinked up at me. I glanced at the mud sliding down the tire where Muffy had pissed like a racehorse instead of a greyhound.

I winced before I turned around to face the music. Holy . . . My arm went limp, and I almost dropped the leash. Dark boots. Worn jeans. FDNY T-shirt. Stubbled jaw. Lips in a flat line. *Keep going. Skip the lips, Pepper.*

Reluctantly, I forced my eyes to continue their perusal upward.

Granite jaw. Blazing brown pools. *Whoa, he was mad.* Mussed dark hair. *Had he just rolled out of bed? No, it was almost dark. He couldn't have. Unless . . . someone else he'd rolled out of bed with had done it . . .*

Muffy nudged my hand.

I stared at the fireman, the George Strait song spinning in my head.

Lick.

I looked down.

Muffy nosed my pocket.

Jolted, I dug out a treat and offered it to him. "Good boy."

"You *praised* your dog for pissing on my truck?" A dark eyebrow rose.

I wanted to sink into the snow-covered sidewalk. Instead, I motioned toward the jacked-up pickup. "He cleaned half your tire. You're welcome."

Inwardly, I cringed. That was so not what I meant to say. *I'm sorry* would've been the correct response, yet I still couldn't find those words.

Lightning flashed in his dark eyes. I inched my neck toward him. *Are those gold flecks in his irises?* Damn, too far away to tell.

"Excuse me?"

I circled my finger in the air toward the tire. "It's filthy. A wash in any capacity is a step in the right direction."

He glared.

I glared back, despite that he could snap me in half with those arms. Why had I turned down the last fireman who'd come by Grey Paws to sell a fundraising calendar? I'd bought a couple, I just hadn't taken the calendars.

You thought it was degrading to men.

Well, I was wrong. Because if he was Mr. January—or any month—I'd sorely missed out.

"Are you justifying what your dog did?" The biceps I'd been admiring bulged when he folded his arms.

"Muffy doesn't see a difference between your tire and that tree." I gestured toward the Callery pear tree on the edge of the sidewalk.

"She should—wait a second." He tilted his head. Muffy mimicked him as they stared at one another. "That's not a she."

"No, he's not."

Muffy wagged his tail, and I patted him on the head.

"You named him Muffy?" Mr. January asked incredulously.

"What's wrong with his name?" Why didn't I just explain how Muffy came to be Muffy?

"He's a greyhound. He's a male. He shouldn't be named Muffy."

"I'll let you tell that to Benjamin."

"Who's Benjamin?"

"The six-year-old who was volunteering with his mother the day we rescued this dog."

At least if I'd had this man in a calendar to ogle he couldn't have talked back. Benjamin had been thrilled to name the dog, like it had been Christmas and his birthday at the same time. Who was I to tell him he couldn't call him Muffy?

Mr. January held up both hands. "Look—"

"No, you look." His lips parted and even Muffy blinked up at me in surprise. "It's freezing, and I don't like cold weather. I give him a treat when he comes outside and does his business fast. All he did was what I asked."

"You told him to piss on my truck?" The tension ramped up another notch instead of diffusing.

"I told him to be quick. It's not like he meant it as a personal insult. He just picked a spot and went." I shrugged. Muffy wagged his tail even faster.

Mr. January scowled. "Don't let it happen again."

He shouldered past me and opened the driver's side door.

"The chances of that happening are about zero, considering you'll never get this parking spot again."

It was right in front of the rescue. I'd worked there twelve years. Never seen the truck before today. Wouldn't ever see it or Mr. January again.

He smirked and pointed at Muffy. "Find another spot to go."

Muffy swiped his big tongue over his finger. Mr. January kept his hard gaze on the dog, but I swore one corner of his mouth lifted.

When those piercing eyes met mine, they were all fire. Nope. The man was a grouch.

"Want us to wash it?" I asked sweetly as he climbed in the cab.

"That would be a start."

Seriously? That truck looked like he'd been driving in a muddy cotton field all day. And by the way, there were no cotton fields in this city last I checked.

"I'll let you know when I want it done."

"The tire. That's—" *Slam.* Did he just shut the door while I was talking? "All I'm washing," I yelled as he cranked up the diesel engine.

Muffy jumped at the noise, and I crouched to comfort him.

Mr. January gunned away from the curb. Just as he swerved into traffic, I caught a glimpse of his license plate.

I ♥ Cher.

CHAPTER TWO

PEPPER

"WHAT WAS THAT RACKET?"

Miss Adeline sat behind the reception desk, her weathered hands absently running over the heads of not one, but two dogs.

"Mr. January," I muttered.

"Thought you got lost. Speedy Gonzales there usually is in and out." The wrinkles around her eyes tightened. "And you said those calendars were degrading."

Old Eagle Ears didn't miss a thing even though she was eighty-three.

"They are."

"Then how'd you recognize Mr. January?"

"How'd you get the calendars? I told the man to keep them." I shot an accusatory look in her direction.

"And I told him to hand them over. No reason to let good money go to waste."

I put a hand on my forehead. Muffy jumped up, his wet paws streaking down the front of my shirt.

"You know he likes to have his feet dried off immediately," Miss Adeline said.

I burst out laughing as she tossed me a towel. "Where are the calendars?" I wiped off one paw as Muffy stood there obediently. "You are such a good boy."

Lick.

Right in the face.

Miss Adeline opened a drawer and pulled out a calendar. She thumbed it open and held it up. "Is that him?"

"You've been keeping that in the reception desk?"

She looked at me like I'd lost my mind. "Hell, yes. One upstairs and one down here." I tried to hold in my laugh, some weird-sounding snort escaping. "Next year buy a few more, so I don't have to carry them around."

"I'm not buying more calendars."

"Maybe I'll be here when that nice young boy comes around selling them again," she muttered.

"You could just go to the fire station. I'm sure they'd be more than happy to sell you all the calendars you want." I wiped off Muffy's last paw, and he took off toward Miss Adeline.

He nosed his way between the other two dogs, and she gave him a treat.

"He just had one," I said, though I wasn't mad.

"Now he's had another."

"Woman . . ."

She pointed at the image of a shirtless fireman holding a hose. "Is this him?"

"I have to feed the dogs."

"It won't kill you to look at a picture."

She shook it, and I sighed. "Fine. That's not him." I folded the damp towel. "And I don't even know if he's a fireman. They sell those FDNY shirts in Times Square."

Miss Adeline leaned forward. "Did he look like a fireman?"

I threw my hands up. "I don't know. What does a fireman look like?"

"This." She tapped her finger on the man in the photo.

"He looked better," I mumbled.

Her eyes lit, and I clinched. Instead of putting an end to this conversation, I'd just thrown fuel on it.

She flipped the page. "Him?"

The next guy was sliding down the pole. "No."

"Him?"

"Are we going through the whole calendar?"

"There's only ten more. Now is this him?"

"Nooo."

Bark. Bark. Bark.

I didn't need to check my watch, knowing it was close enough to six for Sadie to start.

"She can wait three minutes," Miss Adeline said, rolling onto June. "Him?"

"She'll bark until we feed her supper."

Some of her friends in the kennels had joined in. The girl had done that the five years we'd had her. When it was time to eat, she barked. And barked. And barked. She wouldn't stop until her bowl was in front of her.

"That dog could learn some patience," she huffed, though Sadie was Miss Adeline's favorite. Maybe it was because they were so alike. Stubborn. Said what they thought. Had to be in charge.

"She won't learn it from you."

"I get no respect around here."

I froze when she held up October. She turned the calendar back toward herself, and I grabbed it. That half smirk and those lightning eyes stared up at me from the page.

"Ding. Ding. Ding. We have a winner." Miss Adeline sounded downright triumphant. "And he didn't get a knockoff shirt from Times Square."

I slammed the glossy pages shut. "Aren't firemen supposed to be kind?"

"All the ones I've met are."

I spun to find one of our most supportive volunteers in the doorway, a thick binder in her arms.

"Hey, Vivian."

"Is that the FDNY calendar?" She dropped the binder on the desk and picked up the calendar I'd just thrown there.

"The one and only," Miss Adeline said. "And our girl here just met Mr. October."

"I didn't even tell you—"

"Didn't have to." Miss Adeline leaned back in her chair.

Bark. Bark. Bark.

"Why haven't you fed Sadie?" Vivian asked without looking up.

"Because we were appreciating the hard muscles—I mean work— of the fire department." Miss Adeline's old lips formed into a mischievous grin.

I closed my eyes and prayed for strength, even as I felt my own smile form. "I'm going to feed the dogs now."

"She thinks appreciating what God gave us to look at is above her," Miss Adeline said as I walked toward the kennels.

"I do not," I called.

"Do too."

That woman. Life wouldn't be nearly as entertaining without her. We gave each other a hard time like an old married couple, but I adored her. *She rescued me.*

"You met this guy?" Vivian shook the calendar at me as I scooped dog food into a bowl.

"Yeah."

Bark. Bark. Bark.

She let out a low whistle I barely heard as I set Sadie's dinner down in front of her. Her shrill barks turned into chomping. She'd been here the longest and thought she was in charge.

Bark. Bark. Bark.

"Oh, so you've taught Flash your ways?" I asked, but she didn't even look up as she devoured her food.

Her neighbor continued to bark his head off, so I fixed his supper next. I'd tried early on to teach Sadie that barking like that made her be served last. It hadn't mattered. So I'd figured out it was best to just feed her first.

Flash apparently picked up on it after being here only a few days.

Two down, nine more to go.

"Want me to find out what station he works at?" Miss Adeline hollered.

"You could help me feed the dogs," I called back.

"How'd you meet him? Where is he taking you?"

I paused mid-scoop. "I met him outside, and he's not taking me anywhere."

"Talk louder so I can hear."

"Turn your hearing aid up."

Vivian snickered. "What happened?"

"Muffy peed on his tire."

Her eyes went wide. "No."

"Yes."

"He was marking his territory," Miss Adeline chimed in as she rolled her chair into the doorway.

"Then he owns this whole block and half of Central Park." The kibble tinkled against the metal bowls as I aggressively filled the rest.

"When did this happen?"

"Just before you got here," I said, handing her a couple bowls to serve.

"Damn. I missed the good stuff." She placed the bowls in front of the hungry dogs, who sucked up their dinner like vacuums. "Sorry I can't take you for a walk," she said to the dogs. "I came by to tell you the venue is set for the adoption event. Muriella found the perfect park and Daniel leased it. But if it rains, he has a warehouse space lined up."

"Thanks." I surveyed the kennels. Each and every one of these dogs was special. I loved them and would keep them as long as they needed our help. The event was important, and I appreciated Vivian recruiting her best friend and husband to help. But we'd never done anything like a mass adoption. I wasn't sure I was ready for an empty rescue. "I hope people fall in love with them."

"I still think we should have an event here too, but this will get some of these guys where they belong."

"We're at capacity." It was shameful how these animals were

treated once they'd served their purpose. Just because they couldn't race anymore didn't mean they should be discarded like trash.

"I know." Vivian and her husband, Daniel, not only volunteered their time, but some months they were the reason we were able to keep going financially.

She kissed Miss Adeline on top of the head. "Behave."

"That's no fun."

Vivian picked up her binder and disappeared out the door. I locked it behind her.

"She appreciates a nice-looking gentleman," Miss Adeline said.

"So do you . . . although can you see that calendar?"

She harrumphed and slowly got to her feet. "I need a lift."

"Where?"

"The fire station."

CHAPTER THREE

TEAGUE

"WHY DOES it look like you washed off half a tire?"

I punched Cassano in the arm as I slung my bag over my shoulder.

"I thought you were off today."

"No such luck, compadre. Twenty-four more on."

The alarm bell went off and we ran toward the station. Everyone inside buzzed as we threw on our gear and loaded into the truck.

"Three alarm. Residential. Engine Three and Ladder One also headed to the scene."

A buzz rushed through my veins. Fifteen years, thousands of calls, and it was the same every single time.

"Hollingsworth, Cassano, you'll secure the inside. Everyone else, let's make sure this bitch doesn't spread," Burke said from the front seat.

I straightened at the call of my name. We bounced down the street, the engine roar nothing compared to the noise in my head.

Oxygen.

Gloves.

Mask.

Radio.

Mentally, I checked off what I needed before I raced inside.

Three blocks out, the orange glow of the fire lit the night sky. The siren wailed as we pulled to a stop in front of the townhouse.

I jumped out of the truck first. "Stand back, please," I said to the crowd who had gathered. "Anyone know how many inside?"

"Two," someone shouted. "I tried to go in, but there's so much smoke."

"Ready to do this?" Cassano asked as he grabbed his axe.

"Yeah."

Pop. Pop. Pop.

Glass shattered and rained on our heads.

"Everybody get back now!"

Cassano and I ran toward the front door.

"You know we're gonna find marshmallows," he said before he heaved the axe through the door.

I bristled as I shouldered past him through the open door. "You're a sick bastard."

He laughed and followed me into the smoke.

I turned on my light, straining to see through the thick black around us.

"Anybody here?" I shouted.

No response.

We continued on the first level.

"I'll go upstairs," Cassano said as the fire crackled.

"No. We stay together."

"If we don't split up, we *will* find marshmallows."

"*We stay together.*"

I'd been with the department ten years longer than Cassano and what I said went. Besides, it was the smart thing to do in smoke this thick.

Mercifully, he didn't argue as we cleared the living room and a study.

We pressed deeper into the house. Sweat dripped from my forehead into my eye. I blinked a few times to clear the sting.

Heat.

Flames.

The intensity grew with every step we took. I'd seen enough fires to know they were all unpredictable, but my guess was we were close to the source.

"Hollingsworth, what's your status?"

"Two rooms clear downstairs," I responded in the radio.

"We'd have more done if I'd gone up—"

Snap. Crack.

The ceiling above us collapsed. I ducked and shielded my head with my arms but landed on my back. My light was knocked out of my hands.

God, this is heavy.

Weight on my chest and stomach made it hard to breathe. I couldn't see through the dust and smoke.

I shoved, and there was little give in whatever was on top of me.

Not today. Not. Today.

With all my strength, I pushed and somehow got the object off of me. I sat up, ignoring the soreness down my middle.

"Cassano!"

I waited a second and got to my feet.

No response.

"Cassano!"

Nothing.

I took a step forward and immediately ran into something. The only light was from the flames. I strained to see as I felt around. It wasn't a person blocking my path.

Something pliant.

With dips and valleys.

Mattress.

Shit. If I threw it forward, it could hit him. Backward, I'd block our path out.

"Cassano!"

Still silent.

The fire from the back of the house inched closer, spurred by the part that reached upstairs and collapsed the floor.

I tossed the mattress toward it. The box spring followed.

Underneath, in the center, there was a heaping form with a familiar yellow reflective tape.

"Cassano."

He didn't move as I pulled at the slats pinning him. Screwed in? Son of a bitch. He had the axe.

I yanked on one. Those suckers were in tight.

Cough. Cough.

"Cassano? You with me?"

"Hollingsworth?" His voice held none of the swagger it had a few minutes ago. He sounded dazed.

"You would have a bed land on you," I said, trying to distract him. "If you wanted my attention, you didn't have to go this far."

Orange and blue streaks of fire licked closer. He lolled his head toward the flames.

"Asshole," he wheezed out. "When we're out of here, I'm going to—"

The ceiling behind us gave way. I didn't have time to pull out the slats to free him.

I cupped my hand under the frame and used all my strength to lift. It barely budged. One of the posters was wedged against the wall.

Heat.

Sweat.

Flames.

The intensity of the fire raged closer.

"Go. If you don't get out of here, we'll both die."

"I'm not letting you be a marshmallow," I gritted out.

I repositioned my hands, centered myself, and used everything I had to lift. It toppled over. The fire engulfed the wood, sending embers toward the sky.

"Can you sit up?"

Cassano attempted to move. "Ahh." His cry of pain was consumed by the fire.

If I moved him, I could hurt him worse. There was no time for assessment. If I didn't move him, he'd die.

I scooped him up bridal style. "Jesus, lay off the cheesecake."

"Son of a bitch."

Running on pure adrenaline, I stepped over debris and avoided embers as I retraced our path. When I could see the flashing red lights of the fire truck, I picked up my pace. My foot hit something when I was almost to the door. The curled-up form didn't move.

"Hollingsworth, what happened in there?" Captain Koker barked as I emerged from the townhouse.

I ignored him and took Cassano to the ambulance that had arrived on scene. The EMTs scrambled to set up a stretcher. I deposited him on it and marched back toward the house.

"Hollingsworth. I asked you a question."

With determination, I jogged up the short steps, despite the pain in my stomach.

"Hollingsworth! You can't go back in there."

Everything turned to white noise as I retraced my path to whatever had blocked it near the door. I barely glanced at the flames that had almost reached the front of the home, focused solely on finding out what I'd almost tripped on.

It could've been a pillow, but I couldn't sleep if I'd left someone behind who could be saved.

In seconds, I found the form in the same spot. *Thank God, I came back.*

There was no movement, but when I cradled the form against me, I felt a slow up and down of breaths.

"Hollingsworth—"

Captain was still yelling at me when I came out for a second time. Out of the smoke, I finally saw what was in my arms.

A greyhound.

CHAPTER FOUR

TEAGUE

"YOU BROKE protocol going back into that house on your own."

I winced as I stripped off my shirt.

"Are you listening to me?" Captain asked when I opened the shower door.

"If you want an apology, it's not coming."

I dropped my pants and stepped into the stall.

"I want you to follow orders. Cassano nearly died tonight."

I ducked my head under the cold spray in a desperate attempt to drown him out. He hadn't seen him pinned under that bed. If anyone knew just how close Cassano had come to death tonight, it was me.

"I want a full report. Though you probably went rogue in there. When Cassano is out of the hospital, I'm going to find out."

"If I hadn't followed protocol we'd both be dead," I growled.

"When I find out otherwise, you're done."

I closed my eyes and refrained from punching the tiled wall or opening the door and punching him in the face. His assertions I did the wrong thing by Cassano weren't warranted. Never mind I'd saved a dog too.

"Anything else, *Captain?*"

"Yeah. You're suspended without pay for a week."

I slammed the door open. "What?"

My shout drew the attention of the other guys in the bathroom.

"You heard me. After you've showered, go home."

"You can't—"

"Already have."

I hit the wall. Pain radiated from my knuckles up my arm. Captain knew how devoted I was to the station; I did what was necessary to protect our own and the people of this city. Sometimes that meant breaking protocol because sometimes protocol didn't make a damn bit of sense.

If he'd expected me to leave that dog to die, maybe the job I'd sacrificed everything for was the wrong one for me.

I yanked my towel off the door and roughly dried off. When I stepped out of the shower with it tucked around my waist, four of my brothers-in-arms were waiting.

"It's total bullshit," Walsh said.

I grunted my agreement.

"You saved Cassano's ass and that's the thanks you get?" Rivera chimed in. "That ain't right."

"Yo." Burke slapped my shoulder. "You good for the week?"

I swallowed hard. He had three kids and another on the way. It took every penny he made to get by, yet he was willing to help me out financially if I needed it.

"I'm good," I said gruffly.

"Nobody's going to miss your sorry ass." Burke grinned. "It'll be nice to have a week off from your cooking."

"I'm a damn good cook, and you know it." I pointed at him, some of the tension inside loosening.

These guys had my back. They were the ones who mattered. Captain might have rank, but that didn't mean he automatically had our respect.

"DR. LYONS."

"How's the greyhound from the fire?" I was parked near the

station, drumming my fingers of one hand on the steering wheel while holding my phone in the other.

"She had severe smoke inhalation. I'm keeping her overnight, but she should be good tomorrow," the veterinarian said matter-of-factly before her tone softened. "She's a tough girl, and she'll be in good hands."

I furrowed my brow. "Did someone claim her?" Once we'd extinguished the fire, we'd found two people inside who'd passed away. Not that it helped, but upon initial examination, it appeared they were already deceased when we'd arrived.

According to neighbors, the couple and their dog were the only residents of the townhome.

"No. I contacted Grey Paws. They normally rescue greyhounds who were abandoned by their owners once they can no longer race, but they'll do anything for a dog in need."

Grey Paws? Grey Paws? Why did that sound familiar?

At least the poor girl would have somewhere to go, though the thought of her in a shelter didn't sit well with me. She'd not only almost died, but she'd lost the people she loved. That had to be traumatic.

"If anything changes let me know. I'll come by and pay the bill tomorrow."

"Will do. And this one's on the house."

"Thanks."

I hung up and tossed my phone in the cupholder. No sooner than it landed, "Gypsys, Tramps & Thieves" began. The guys at the station thought it was funny to change my ringtone to different Cher songs all the time.

"What's up, big brother?" I answered as soon as I saw the caller ID.

"Were you in that fire up on West Twenty-ninth? I heard there was a firefighter hospitalized."

"I've got a hot nurse by my bed right now giving me personal attention, but you interrupted."

"That's not funny."

Maybe it wasn't, especially given that Cassano was the one in the hospital, but joking was the only way I knew how to cope.

"She says she'll do *whatever* it takes to make me feel better."

"Teague."

My older brother had always been the serious sort, then again, he'd had to be. And I didn't know what I'd do without him. Lincoln had supported me all my life. While he didn't particularly like that I'd chosen a career where I had to risk my life, he had my back.

"The ceiling collapsed. A bed pinned Cassano down, but I got him out."

"Are you okay?" Laced in my brother's stiff words was worry.

"Yeah." I debated for a minute whether or not to tell him the rest. He'd want to swoop in to fix things, and I appreciated that, but I didn't need him to do my fighting. "Captain suspended me for a week without pay."

"Why?" The anger on my behalf pelted me in the ear, and I was grateful for the support.

"I went back in alone and got a dog out."

"So you saved Cassano's life and a dog, yet you're punished? I'll have him suspended without pay and see how he likes it."

"Don't."

I had no doubt as soon as we were off the phone, my brother would have me reinstated. Hell, I might even be chief by the time he was done.

"The suspension will go on your record."

Along with a few others you don't know about.

"Since my week just opened up, want to hang sometime?" I changed the subject and prayed he'd let it go.

"Dad wants you to come to dinner on Friday," he said quietly.

"He can want in one hand, shit in the other, and see which fills up first," I snapped. It wasn't fair to my brother who was always in the middle, but he knew what an ass our father was. He had to work with him on a daily basis.

"Beau's coming."

"Is she back?"

Playing the sister card was a smart move on Lincoln's part. She'd been in London over a decade and rarely came to New York anymore. The three of us were close. I couldn't help but be a little hurt she hadn't told me, especially since I'd just talked to her a couple days ago.

"Only for the weekend."

I scowled at how short her trip would be.

"At least I've got time off."

CHAPTER FIVE

PEPPER

"MR. OCTOBER."

My hand slipped as I tried to put a leash on our new resident when Miss Adeline made the announcement. I'd heard the front door to the rescue chime. But surely that old woman hadn't gone so far as to track him down?

I stayed crouched by the dog, who didn't move. She just looked up at me with sad eyes. I ached for her loss.

"The one and only." That deep wry tone had me closing my eyes. Except when I did, all I visualized was the man I'd seen yesterday. That seemed to be happening frequently.

Probably because Miss Adeline kept leaving that calendar around open to his month.

"Personally, Mr. December is more my type. They definitely saved the best for last." I covered my mouth to keep from laughing. "But you're not so bad to look at."

"If I tell Walsh you like him the best, his big ego will never deflate."

I recognized the voice. It was definitely the one that belonged to Mr. October. But yesterday, it had been harsh. Today, it was . . . playful?

"You can keep hiding behind the desk, but you're missing out on a hell of a view."

I cringed when Miss Adeline's voice was directed at me. Heat crept through my whole body. Slowly, I stood and faced Mr. October.

Those dark eyes flashed with recognition. "You."

"Did you need the rest of your tires rinsed off?" Crap. I hadn't meant to say that.

Miss Adeline raised a gray brow. She and I ribbed each other all the time, but I didn't do it often with others, especially not people who came to the rescue.

One corner of his mouth twitched, but he kept a straight face.

I held up two leashes. "Muffy's ready for a walk."

At the sound of his name, he leapt up from Ash's side. He hadn't left her since she'd arrived earlier today.

Woof.

He rounded the desk and ran toward Mr. October at full speed.

"Muffy. Don't"—he put his two front paws on Mr. October's stomach—"jump," I finished weakly.

Mr. October winced. I held my breath, waiting for the jerk from yesterday to emerge. Instead, he rubbed down Muffy's sides.

"You are something else, aren't you?"

Muffy wagged his tail and attempted to lick him.

Ash perked up and peeked around the desk. She tilted her head, sniffed a couple of times, and pushed to her feet. Carefully, she moved toward Mr. October with her long gait. She licked his hand.

"Well, hey," he said in a soft tone. If this had been the man I met yesterday, I'd have been goo on the sidewalk.

Miss Adeline looked at me as I watched the scene and her eyes glittered dangerously. I shot her a warning look, which was useless.

Mr. October gently put Muffy's paws back on the floor.

"Looks like he got you dirty. You're going to have to take that shirt off," Miss Adeline said. Good Lord, she was serious. The woman had no tact.

Streaks of water ran down his gray Henley.

"He doesn't just like to drink water." Muffy looked at me like he knew I was talking about him. "He likes to play in it too."

"It'll dry."

"If you take it off, it will."

I elbowed Miss Adeline, and she elbowed me back.

"I'm looking for a dog Dr. Lyons said she brought by earlier. She was in a fire."

I lifted my chin in Ash's direction. "That's her."

His brow furrowed. He stared at the dog and then dropped to a squat. Muffy crawled all over him. He put one arm around him and cupped Ash's face with the other hand.

"You're a pretty girl," he said, and I had to lean on the desk for support. "I didn't recognize you without all that soot on you."

But she'd recognized him. She leaned into his touch.

He put his forehead to hers. "You're so brave."

"She has a burn on her back hindquarters, but Dr. Lyons says it will heal," I said. The wound was about six inches long, but the vet couldn't tell what had caused the burn.

Mr. October examined the bandage for himself. "I'm sorry, baby girl. I hope it doesn't hurt too much."

I'd seen countless volunteers and potential adopters with our greyhounds. None of them had ever made me all fidgety. He was so kind and gentle with Ash, a contradiction to his tough exterior.

Muffy swiped his tongue over Ash's ear. She returned the favor, getting him square in the nose.

"Already made a friend, I see. Hope you don't have a truck or he'll pee on it." Mr. October made himself at home on the floor. Both dogs clamored to get into his lap. Each ended up with a head on one of those long legs.

"We could use a few more volunteers," Miss Adeline said oh-so-helpfully, breaking the spell I was under.

"How many dogs do you have?" He kept his attention on the ones in his lap.

"Eleven," I said.

His brows shot up. "How many people work here?"

Miss Adeline puffed her chest out. "You're looking at them."

"It's not work."

He tilted his head and studied me. Technically, it was a lot of work, but these dogs weren't a job to me. They were my life. How anyone could've discarded them so easily, I'd never understand.

I held his gaze, even though it was uncomfortable. His dark eyes were no less fierce than they'd been the other day, but now, I wasn't exactly sure what was in them. The anger had been a lot easier to take than whatever was there now. It made me want to duck back down behind the desk.

Bark. Bark. Bark.

Mr. October gestured toward the direction the noise came from in the back. "Aren't you going to go see what that's all about?"

Bark. Bark. Bark.

"That's Sadie. She wants her dinner."

"Sounds like it," he said, looking uncertain.

"She doesn't wear a watch, but at six every single morning and night, she demands her meals." Fondness washed over me. It was aggravating at times, but it made her who she was. "If she doesn't bark, that's the time to get worried."

He continued to rub both dogs. "They all have their personalities, don't they?"

"They do." I picked up leashes off the desk. "I'm going to take them outside." Muffy jumped up at the word *outside*. It never ceased to amaze me how intelligent they were.

"You're ready to go." Ash lifted her head, and Mr. October stroked it. "I'll take them. We won't go far."

I hesitated. Why did I always do that? He was a fireman. He'd come by to check on Ash. I doubted he was going to take off and never come back.

I tossed the leashes beside him. "Thanks." *Bark. Bark. Bark.* "I'm going to feed her before she loses her voice."

He laughed, and I was grateful for the desk to support me. After a second, I moved toward the back.

"You should stay for supper. I don't know what we're having yet, but that's irrelevant." I stumbled at Miss Adeline's invitation. We never had anybody over for dinner. We couldn't have *him*. I was still struggling with the fact he was at the rescue and why he made me so damn uncomfortable.

I willed Sadie to be quiet for two seconds so I could hear his answer. *Bark. Bark. Bark.* I craned my neck toward the front and tried to tune out the barking.

"Sure."

Oh my God.

CHAPTER SIX

TEAGUE

"BEST DECISION I made all day. Eye candy and decent food."

The old woman I'd come to know as Miss Adeline shoved mac and cheese into her mouth.

"Decent?" I asked, pretending offense. These two women went back and forth like an old married couple and somehow, I'd fallen right into the mix. Dinner with them reminded me a lot of eating meals at the firehouse.

"Yeah, it's decent."

"She's not going to sugarcoat anything," Pepper said as she hedged around her serving of mac and cheese to the black-eyed peas.

"When you get to be my age, you have to cut through the crap."

Pepper smirked as she took a sip of water. "You definitely excel at that."

Muffy nudged me with his nose, then put his head in my lap. Discreetly, I fed him a bite of chicken. He smacked so loudly, I was busted.

The warning glare Pepper shot me was enough to put a little fear in me. "I noticed you barely touched your mac and cheese," I said to her.

She opened her mouth to respond but Miss Adeline beat her to it.

"She doesn't like it."

Pepper's glare shifted from me to the older woman. "Yours is good . . ."

"You don't have to eat it," I said. That tiny, tentative bite she'd taken earlier made more sense now.

"Unlike some people"—she cut her eyes over to Miss Adeline—"I don't want to be rude."

"It's not rude to not like something," Miss Adeline said as she scarfed down the rest of hers.

"My feelings are only a little hurt," I said with a pout.

Pepper's mouth flattened, making mine turn up. "You were kind enough to make dinner and—"

"Noted. No more mac and cheese on the menu."

Lines creased her forehead.

"Why do I have to suffer because she doesn't like it?" Miss Adeline complained.

"That's a big assumption he's going to cook for you again," Pepper said.

I wiped my mouth with my napkin and leaned back in the chair. "Happy to anytime." Something about making her uncomfortable entertained me.

"I'm sure your job takes up a lot of your time."

I scowled at the reminder that, for the week, I was out of a job. "Yeah."

Her brow furrowed, but instead of saying anything, she tore off a piece of dinner roll and shoved it into her mouth.

Then she raked her portion of mac and cheese onto Miss Adeline's plate, who dug right in. The chair scraped when she pushed back from the table. "Thank you for dinner. It was delicious."

The words sounded as if they were torn from her throat.

"Beats the hell out of the cereal we were going to have."

Pepper marched to the sink without a word and turned on the taps. Muffy got up to see if she was okay. Ash looked over at them, ears back, but she stayed at my feet.

"Excuse me," I said as I stood.

Miss Adeline waved me off as she finished the last bite of her dinner. I pushed my chair in and turned in the small space between where I'd been seated and the wall of cabinets where the sink was.

I pushed up my shirt sleeves and took the fork Pepper had just washed from her fingers.

"You cooked. I'll clean," she snapped.

"I don't mind." I glanced to the lower cabinets and found there was no dishwasher.

The apartment wasn't modern by any means, but it appeared as if it had been updated in the period when the appliance was common.

Miss Adeline was halfway out of her chair when I motioned for her to sit back down. "I'll clear." I gathered the remaining dishes and plates. "Should I cover the leftovers or do you want them in a different container?"

"There are some glass dishes with snap lids in the bottom cabinet there." Miss Adeline pointed to the one just beside Pepper.

I squatted and tried to ignore the close view I had of her shapely ass. There was a stain on her back pocket in the shape of a paw print. *Lucky dog.*

Pepper tapped the cabinet door. "In there. Not my back pocket."

I smirked but easily found the glass containers once I made an effort. "Do the two of you eat together every night?"

"I try to get her to go out on dates, but does she listen? Everybody I set her up with is a bust," Miss Adeline said with disgust.

"I don't need you to set me up," Pepper argued.

"Well, you ain't getting any dates on your own."

Interesting.

"Maybe I don't want any."

"Twelve years I've known this one." Miss Adeline jabbed an old finger toward Pepper. "The only time we're not together is when she's walking the dogs, shopping, taking a bath, and sleeping. If she's gotten laid during any of that, she's redefined the meaning of quickie."

And this lady had mastered the art of brutal honesty. Pepper washed the plate in her hand aggressively.

"I'm standing right here."

"And I'm trying to tell Mr. October here that you're practically a virgin. At least twelve years celibate counts as a clean slate, if you ask me."

"I didn't."

"I have to agree," I said, scooping the leftovers into the containers.

"Nobody asked you either," Pepper said.

How could she not have dated in twelve years? It sounded as if it was by her own choice, but I didn't understand.

She was beautiful in a simple, understated way. Minimal makeup. Dark hair piled in a high ponytail on top of her head. Jeans and a sweatshirt that appeared well-worn.

Gray eyes that turned a smoky shade when she got mad. Lips that were impossible not to notice, especially when they turned up.

And she had a sharp wit. When she'd asked me if I wanted Muffy to rinse off the rest of the tire, it had taken all my composure not to laugh. But I'd been irritated by a message from my father. She and Muffy had received the brunt of it.

She scrubbed a serving dish. When she was finished, I took it and rinsed before I set it on the towel laid out to dry it.

"I bet you don't have too many dates with a license plate like yours." There was fire behind her words, but I understood. Nobody liked to be ribbed even when it came from a good place. Miss Adeline wanted her to be happy. That much was obvious.

And I was used to taking shit for my truck tag. I was well past the point of being upset about it.

"Women dig sensitive men."

She paused mid-wipe. "Dig?"

"Yeah. Dig."

"Are you going to the concert that's coming up?" Miss Adeline asked.

Pepper blushed. Sounded like somebody had been talking about me.

"Nah. Tickets are hard to come by." *Not that I'd tried.*

"I know a guy." She shrugged.

"Somehow, I don't doubt that."

CHAPTER SEVEN

PEPPER

"HOW DID I MISS THIS BALCONY?"

Mr. October stood frozen in the doorway that led outside. Miss Adeline's apartment was massive by most New York standards at nearly two thousand square feet. It spanned the top floor of the three-story Grey Paws building, and at times it felt even larger because of the twenty-foot ceilings.

"I told my Hastings I wanted a balcony." Miss Adeline brushed some snow off her rocking chair and sat down.

"How'd you find one in this city?"

I pressed the starter on the gas heater situated between our two usual chairs, but it didn't ignite.

Mr. October reached around me and got it going with one try.

"Thanks," I said as I sat.

He settled in the chair beside me.

"We built it," Miss Adeline said. She pulled her toboggan lower over her ears.

"I beg your pardon."

"The building that used to be here was in shambles. We bought it. Rebuilt. I wanted a balcony we could sit on every morning and every evening. And my husband didn't say no to me."

I'd heard so many stories about Hastings Gidrey I felt like I knew the man. But he'd passed away of a heart attack a few years before Miss Adeline and I met.

"Does anybody say no to you?" I pressed my foot to the floor and began to rock. "What are these chairs made out of anyway? You've had them longer than we've known each other."

"Hastings built them when we moved here sixty years ago."

They were worn and weathered, but somehow, they'd withstood the test of time. I suggested getting some new ones once before I knew Miss Adeline's late husband had made them. It didn't go over well.

"Was he a carpenter?" Mr. October asked. When was he going to tell us his name? Better yet, why hadn't I asked?

"He did a little of this and that." She leaned her head on the back of the rocking chair and looked up at the stars.

Muffy and Ash curled up on the blanket we'd brought out for them. Most nights, when it was warmer, we let all the dogs up here so they felt like they were in a home instead of a rescue center.

"How'd you start rescuing dogs?

Miss Adeline snorted. "We were at a racetrack in Miami. I wanted to see the dogs after the race, so we went to the kennels. One of them had broken his leg. They were about to shoot him like he was useless. I stood between Sunshine and the gun. There were two more they were going to put down because they couldn't race anymore. After that, I was determined to save as many as I could."

That was over fifty years ago, and by now, things should have been different—humanity should have been—but greyhounds who could no longer race were treated worse than trash. Miss Adeline insisted upon going to every rescue we went on. She might be old, but I'd seen her do what it took to save the dogs.

"Tell him about the ride home," I said, trying to hide my smile.

"We had a fifty-four Ford we'd driven down. Once we had those dogs, it was like they knew we'd saved them. I opened the passenger side door and all three of them went for the front." She snickered. "I grabbed the keys from Hastings after I helped Sunshine in the car and my husband had to sit in the backseat all the way back to New York. He said it was nice to be chauffeured. But by the time we were home, we had four more dogs."

"What did you do with seven dogs? This is a nice apartment, but that would get cramped fast," Mr. October said incredulously.

"We'd talked for a couple years about what to do with the downstairs space. We went back and forth about renting it, even had a few people want to put a restaurant in. But we never committed because we didn't want the noise below us. As soon as we had the dogs, I knew why we'd never done anything with it. We were waiting for the dogs to come home."

"Did you keep all of them?"

She laughed. "We did. It was a circus."

"So how did the two of you meet?" His penetrating gaze landed on me. "Were you a volunteer?"

Tension, thick and fierce tightened every muscle in my body. Miss Adeline reached over and patted my hand, which helped.

"I was at a track in Virginia. They were abusing the dogs. I found a letter Miss Adeline mails to all the tracks to tell them any dog they don't want, she'll come get." I swallowed hard.

"She called, I went."

It wasn't just the dogs she'd picked up that day.

"YOU THE ONE *who called me about the dogs?*"

The woman was way older than she'd sounded on the phone. But she had a van. I could help her get them in it.

I hiked my backpack on my shoulders and looked around. "Yes."

A determination filled her eyes. "Then let's get to it. Hop on in."

I shook my head and glanced down the road toward the track . . . which was too far away to see. "I'll walk back."

"Honey, if you trust me to rescue those dogs, you can trust me to give you a ride."

I shook my head again and took a step back. "I unlocked the back gate. Take the first drive before the main entrance and I'll open it for you."

She assessed my dirty overalls and messy hair. I'd washed my face in the gas station bathroom while I'd waited, but I was still gross.

"Lead the way."

I took off, staying as far away from the edge of the pavement on the busy road as I could get. It was early, but the June sun already blazed. Sweat misted my forehead. I swiped away a drop as it trickled down my cheek. A dirt streak was left down my arm. Crap. Probably had that on my face now.

I moved as fast as I could. Once I was almost to the back entrance of the racetrack, I slipped into the tree line. Even in the shade, the thick humid air made it hard to breathe.

When I could see the gate, I peered to make sure the lock was as I'd left it before I emerged from the woods. The chain was secured, but the padlock was unlatched.

I scurried to loosen the chain, careful to stay quiet. I froze when a golf cart in the distance inside the fence whizzed by. I exhaled heavily when it kept going.

Creak.

I swung the gate open.

The van crept down the road toward me.

Thump. Thump. Thump.

My heartbeats thundered in my ears. The dogs were so close to being saved. At least I prayed I'd made the right call.

The brakes squealed when the van rolled to a stop just inside the gate. I closed it and fixed the chain so it appeared to be locked again.

This is for the dogs.

I shoved down my nerves, opened the passenger side door, and climbed inside. "That way." I pointed to the kennels.

The old woman gunned it across the parking lot. "You can leave your backpack in here."

"No," I snapped quickly, hanging on to the straps for dear life.

She kept driving, unbothered by my outburst. "How many people will be around?"

"There shouldn't be any. The handlers started working the first group about a half hour ago." I pointed again. "Stop here. Let me make sure it's clear."

She released a grunt of agreement.

I hopped out and slid a window up on the back side of the building. They locked the doors but never this window. It was an easy in and out. I shimmied inside. The scent of dogs hit my nose the way it always did. I couldn't ever exactly describe the smell . . . only that it was home.

I waited a beat and listened.

The dogs had barked like mad the first few times I came in and out, but they didn't make a sound now. I crept to the row of kennels.

Lola was curled up, her body jerking with unsteady breaths. I unlatched her door. She lifted her eyes but not her head, as if the effort were too much.

"You're gonna be safe soon," I promised. I didn't know that old woman in the van, but from the moment we'd spoken on the phone, I'd trusted she could help these poor creatures.

The door swung open, sunlight streaming inside. I froze but exhaled with relief when it was just the old lady.

"Are we doing this today?" Frown lines formed around her eyes when she saw Lola. "Can she walk?"

I shook my head. "I don't think so."

The lady stooped and gently scooped Lola off the floor. How could she pick up a dog of that size? I was less than half her age and it was a struggle. But she marched out to the van, so I opened Jasper's and Finn's kennels.

They followed me out to the van, and we loaded them inside. The two of them went without straying as if they knew we were helping them.

There was no time for goodbye. If we didn't hurry we'd be caught.

I kissed both their noses.

"I could use some help at the rescue," the woman said.

I looked back toward the kennels. What if another dog needed me here? They were my . . . family.

Shrill, sharp barks sounded like crazy from inside. Crap. Someone was in there.

"Let me buy you breakfast and you can think about it," she said as she hurried back into the driver's seat.

She threw the van in gear.

Stay. Go. Stay. Go.

As she backed up, I jumped inside.

.   .   .

"I NEED to go let the dogs out before bed." Abruptly, I got to my feet.

"I'll help," Mr. October said.

"No." I cleared my throat and tried again. "I've got it. I'm sure you need to go home anyway."

"Actually, I don't."

CHAPTER EIGHT

TEAGUE

"YOU TAKE ALL these dogs out every night by yourself?"

Pepper looped a leash around the dog she called Sadie. She wrangled another and made it look easy.

"I do it in the morning and afternoon too," she snapped.

Something had happened upstairs. She hadn't been friendly the entire night, but her mood had darkened.

I took one of the leashes from her hand, and she scowled. "I'll help. It's not safe to be walking around at night."

She snorted. "What do you propose I do? The dogs need exercise and bathroom breaks whether it's safe or not."

"Promise me you won't go out after dark alone anymore."

Her back was to me, but I didn't miss the way she stiffened. "I can't do that."

I followed her—more like was dragged by two excited greyhounds —out the front door of the rescue. She locked it behind us as if she was empty-handed instead of handling two dogs of her own.

As soon as they heard the lock click, they shot off down the sidewalk. "Easy, guys. It's slick out."

I caught up to her. The four dogs pranced with their noses

working overtime. They seemed to know where they were going, while I was along for the ride.

"Should I let them hose down your truck?" She pointed her chin toward my parked vehicle.

"As I recall, you owe me a wash." I bumped her shoulder and a mischievous curve shaped her lips.

"Why is your truck so muddy anyway?" she asked as we continued in perfect rhythm down the sidewalk.

"Went to Jersey to do some training." Sadie stopped to sniff. "By the way, you're not getting out of washing my truck." I smirked. "Especially since I cooked dinner for you."

"If I'd have had it my way, you wouldn't have," she muttered.

We continued down the street in silence for a few minutes. A couple stopped to let us pass since we took up the whole sidewalk. Another man went around through the parked cars.

"Why don't you date?"

She whipped her head around. "Excuse me?"

"You heard me. Why. Don't. You. Date?"

With every enunciation, her scowl deepened.

"That's none of your concern," she said shortly.

"I don't date that much either," I volunteered. She looked at me skeptically. "Crazy hours. Dangerous job. Dirty truck." I attempted to lighten the mood, but she didn't crack a smile.

"Sounds like you date your job."

"Looks like you do too."

"This isn't a job for me," she said, her voice reverent.

Images of the way she treated the dogs and Miss Adeline flashed through my head. What little I'd seen, she behaved like they were everything.

Then it occurred to me being a firefighter wasn't just a job for me either. It was a calling. While part of me had cooked dinner for Pepper and Miss Adeline just to get under Pepper's skin, I'd done it to keep myself occupied because I should've been doing it for the guys at the station tonight.

Anger bubbled up. I'd serve this suspension. There was no point in fighting through the bureaucracy bullcrap that might get me sidelined even longer. But if Captain thought I'd take this quietly, he didn't know me well. And he should. He'd held the position thirteen of my fifteen years. I followed orders I believed in but wasn't afraid to buck the system. Our relationship had been strained the entire time because of that.

One of Pepper's dogs jetted forward. She stumbled but didn't fall. "Oscar. Easy. I know we're almost there."

She was so good with them. Patient. Kind. She spoke to them as if they understood. Judging by the way Oscar slowed his gait, maybe they did.

"So that's Oscar. And that's Sadie." I lifted one of the leashes in my hands. "I know Muffy and Ash. But who else do we have?"

That skeptical look was back. Like she didn't want to bother because I'd just forget later.

"You haven't exactly introduced yourself either," she said.

"You've been dying to know my name, haven't you? And here I thought you were content to continue calling me Mr. October."

"Miss Adeline is," she muttered.

I'd never been a fan of the photo shoot for the calendar. The photographers always had us in the weirdest positions. We were oiled down, shirtless—always—and had to hold the hoses and other things nothing like we'd hold them if on the job. But Miss Adeline calling me Mr. October had been amusing, and Pepper's irritation by it even funnier.

"Teague. I like to go on long walks, prepare gourmet meals, and rescue cats."

Oscar jerked his head around at the word *cats*.

Pepper laughed, though I wasn't sure if it was at Oscar or me. "He likes cats too. I'm just not sure rescuing is the right description."

"Milwaukee, but Millie for short." She motioned toward the other dog in my grasp. "And Jet."

And there were nine more dogs. That was a lot to keep up with, especially for one person.

"How often do you call one of them the wrong name?" I strolled beside her, fascinated with how easy she made this look.

Sadie stopped to sniff a food wrapper that had been discarded on the sidewalk. I paused to pick it up, but Jet kept moving. As my arms stretched in two directions, I felt like Gumby.

Sadie wouldn't let go of the hamburger wrapper and Jet had picked up speed as another dog approached. I tugged on the leash, but that only made him more excited.

The paper ripped in half. Part of it was in my fist, along with Sadie's leash, the other dangling from her mouth.

"Teague," Pepper said urgently.

Jet was almost to the approaching Yorkie. The man walking the dog scooped him up just before he reached them.

He cradled the small fur ball and nuzzled him. And then sent a death glare in my direction. "You need to control that beast."

"You're a dog owner. You should understand sometimes they get excited," I said as Jet stared up at the Yorkie, panting.

The man muttered something under his breath and scooted past. Jet looked after them, like he couldn't understand why they'd left.

Pepper gaped at me.

I saved people from burning buildings, but walking two dogs at a time had proved to be too much for me.

"You took up for Jet?" she asked in disbelief.

"Of course I did. He's just curious." I shrugged and attempted to get the paper still dangling from Sadie's mouth.

She backed up.

I followed.

She took another step back.

I managed to get a corner of the wrapper, but most of it remained in her mouth.

Then she pranced forward, and Jet fell in step. I had no choice but to follow.

Pepper, Oscar, and Millie joined us.

"But yesterday. You were so mad at Muffy."

I looked toward Pepper. Her hair was a disaster. She had a stain on the side of her shirt I hadn't noticed before that I really couldn't be sure what it was. Kinda looked green. There were deep-set lines around her eyes. Yet she hadn't complained once about being tired when it was obvious she was.

"Umm . . ." She pointed to Jet, who had wound his way around a streetlamp pole.

I managed to untangle him, while Sadie looked on with that wrapper still in her mouth like she was taunting me.

"I'm sorry," I said. "I'd just gotten off a bad phone call and took it out on the two of you. It won't happen again."

Pepper nodded once. "Apology accepted."

Some sort of weight I didn't realize was bearing down on me lifted.

I wasn't normally a jerk, but there were times after an especially long shift that I was less patient than others. Add in a call from my father? I had wronged Pepper, though, and it was right to apologize. Right for her too if the surprise in her eyes was anything to go by.

I grinned. "But you still owe me a truck wash."

CHAPTER NINE

TEAGUE

"WHAT'S UP, BIG BROTHER?"

I smacked Lincoln on the shoulder and tossed my gym bag on the bench beside him.

"You're early."

"By five minutes."

"Might as well be an hour for you." He tied his sneaker and stood. "How are you holding up?"

Considering yesterday Pepper had distracted me and today I was playing basketball with my brother, I hadn't had a lot of time to dwell on the suspension.

"Not bad," I answered honestly. "Dad let you out of work for a morning?" The bitterness that always laced my voice when I spoke of our father was no less present now. I hated that he elicited any kind of emotion from me, but I couldn't stop it.

"It's Sunday."

"Since when does that matter? The company comes first." Tension tightened my shoulders. I willed them to relax to no avail.

"You gentlemen going to play or stand around and chitchat all day?" Daniel Elliott strolled in, twirling his key ring around his finger.

"That trash talk isn't going to help you win." I slapped hands with him.

"Your jump shot isn't going to help you either," he fired back as he playfully punched me in the stomach. I winced. He hadn't hit me hard, but I was still sore. "I barely touched you." There was apology and worry on his face.

I lifted my shirt. His eyes bulged at the bruise across my stomach.

"A beam fell on me," I said proudly.

"Shit, man. That looks vicious."

My brother circled around to examine me for himself. He scowled. "Have you had someone look at this?"

"Nah. It'll heal." I'd avoided having the paramedics on scene look at my injury. That was the one break in protocol Captain didn't seem to mind. I waved my hand toward the court. "Are we going to do this?"

I grabbed a ball from the rack and dribbled toward the basket, executing a perfect layup. It didn't feel great on my sore stomach, but I could get through it.

Daniel scooped up the basketball and ran toward the opposite basket. Lincoln intercepted and stole the ball from his grasp.

"Not bad for an old guy," Daniel said, hustling after my brother.

"I'm a year younger than you." He paused, took a three-point shot, and the ball whooshed through the net.

"And I'm not forty yet," I taunted, though I was close. That earned a lethal glare from them, who were both over that hump.

Daniel took his own shot and scored. "It's been a while but looks like none of us are rusty." He passed the ball to me. "Your brother has his own court to practice so it's no wonder he drilled that three-pointer."

Lincoln's face turned a deeper shade of red that wasn't from working up a sweat. He was the most confident man I knew, yet flashing his wealth made him uncomfortable, even around people who had money of their own.

"And you're on that court right now. So keep talking. I'll keep scoring," he said as he swiped the ball from me.

"No mercy for your own brother?" I complained as I chased him.

"Nope." But that was a lie. Maybe not in a fun game of basketball, but in everything else, he was my rock.

"At least I know you two won't team up against me."

We'd been friends with Daniel for a few years. He and Lincoln hit it off over a business deal and were close. I was part of that by extension. My brother didn't let people in easily, and that had only gotten worse the older we became. I didn't blame him. We'd learned early on that we'd lose the people we loved.

The ball sailed into my chest and bounced back to Lincoln.

"Where are you?" he asked. "I thought you wanted the ball?"

I shook it off. "Are you trying to give me a cracked rib?" I scooped the basketball up.

"You watched me score. I was showing mercy."

Daniel stepped between us and held up both hands. "Are we going to need to hire a referee next time?"

I took off around him. "Nope. You can referee since you never have the ball."

"Hollingsworth," he shouted as he chased me.

"He shoots." I lined up on the three-point line. "He scores," I yelled as the ball swished through the net. *He curls in a ball in pain.* My stomach felt like an elephant had sat on it.

"I need a break," Lincoln said, tossing both of us a bottle of water.

He'd barely broken a sweat, was in as good a shape as I was even though he sat behind a desk. And he could read me like a book.

"Go get that checked out, little brother," he murmured where only I could hear.

"Vivian and Muriella are organizing a fundraiser and adoption event. I want you both to come." Daniel wiped the cold bottle of water across his forehead.

"In case you haven't noticed, we're both blissfully unattached. I don't think either of us are ready for kids." I lifted my T-shirt to clean the sweat from my face. A punch landed on my arm. "Ow. What was that for?"

"Not kids. Dogs."

I dropped my shirt. "I'd love to have a dog, but are you gonna babysit when I'm at the station?" Muffy, Ash, Sadie, and Jet popped into my head. They were a handful, but hanging around with them had been fun. Actually, it had been more than that. I hadn't had a dog since I was a kid and I'd missed the companionship. Or maybe a certain smoky-eyed creature had more to do with the experience being enjoyable.

Daniel glared at me. "Vivian and Muriella worked hard on this. You don't have to adopt a dog, but a donation and your support would be nice."

"Tell me when and where. I'll be there." Lincoln said.

"I'm in too." I chugged cold water. "What's the shelter?"

"Grey Paws."

I nearly dropped the bottle. Everything in my life seemed to be circling around that rescue lately.

"Well, well. Both of my sons have forgone work to play games. I certainly didn't teach you that."

I jerked my head toward the edge of the court. The last person I wanted to see stood tall in his customary suit and polished dress shoes.

My father.

CHAPTER TEN

TEAGUE

"YOU KNEW HE WAS COMING OVER?"

The question directed at my brother came out as more of an accusatory hiss.

He glared at me. "I wouldn't do that to you."

And what he didn't say was I should trust him more than that.

"I don't like unannounced visits."

"That makes two of us."

Daniel sidled up beside me. "Want me to stay? Referee? Because there is some serious tension going on here."

"No. You shouldn't be involved in family drama," Lincoln said.

Our father waited impatiently in the door to the basketball court. He'd come without warning, yet expected us to hop to his demands.

"Mr. Hollingsworth." Daniel lifted his chin but didn't shake my father's hand before he turned to my brother and me. "Good game. Do it again soon?"

"Soon," I said, doing my best to appear unaffected by the looming presence a few feet away.

Eight months.

That was how long it had been since I'd seen or spoken to the man.

"Call you later," Lincoln said as Daniel held up his phone.

He had barely disappeared when our father started in. "I told you that *career* of yours was a dead end."

Not that I'd expect any concern for my well-being, but if he knew I'd been suspended, he most definitely knew the reason why. Would it have killed him to ask if I was okay?

"I'm out." I spoke to my brother as if our father wasn't there. "Meet me later this week? With Beau?"

It was petty, but I wanted Dad to know we were a family *without* him. We didn't need him. I didn't want him.

"Yeah. She's staying with me when she gets in."

I nodded. At least my sister arriving was good news.

Our father didn't move from where his hulking frame took up the doorway.

"You nearly got a man killed. Did you think of the consequences of that?" He wore that same stern look he'd had all my life. An exterior of stone. "Who do you think that family is going to come after? You'll cost me everything I've worked for while you've been out attempting to play superhero."

Ah. Now the surprise ambush made perfect sense. He was afraid Cassano would sue my family along with the city and whoever else the lawyers thought to throw in. Because I came from money. But it wasn't mine, and it never would be.

Cassano wouldn't do that either. We were brothers too.

"I'm sure you've done more than necessary to shore up your fortune so it's untouchable." I lifted a brow. "Are you finished?"

"It's obvious you have no regard for me, but don't you care about your brother and sister? What they stand to lose? And your mother would be so dis—"

"*Don't* bring her into this," I said, my voice low and guttural.

"That's enough." Lincoln stepped between us. "Teague risked his life to save that man. If it weren't for Teague, he'd be dead."

My brother had always been the steel wall between my father and me. And I was never more grateful, though I hated he had to fight my battles.

"Don't be a fool." My father made a disgruntled noise. "Teague has always been reckless. If it weren't for him—"

"We'll speak when I get to the office," Lincoln said in an authoritative tone.

Dad was none too pleased at being cut off. He flicked his hand at me. "It's time to grow up. You need to join the family business and take some of the burden off your siblings. And be where I can keep a bridle on you before you destroy anything else."

He turned on his heel and disappeared, always the one with the last word.

"Don't worry about him. He'll get over it." Lincoln placed a hand on my shoulder.

"He's had thirty-four years to do that. Sounds like he's just getting warmed up." I looked away. My father's words were like flaming arrows. I'd wondered a thousand times if they would have any effect on me if there was no truth in them. But there was. And they did.

The hurt he inflicted was far worse that the massive bruise on my chest and stomach.

"Beau and I are proud of you for doing what you love. It takes guts to stand up to him. More than I'll ever have," he muttered.

"Oh yeah? From where I'm standing, all you do is stand up to him," I challenged.

"Hello? Is anybody in this monstrosity of an apartment?"

We both looked at each other at the sound of the familiar voice.

"Up here," we said at the same time.

Our sister appeared like a vision. I rushed forward, picked her up, and spun her around.

She squealed and beat on my shoulder. "Put me down, you big oaf."

"Good to see you too, little sister." I grinned and pulled her in for a hug. A bite of pain rushed up my middle.

"Then why did you wince?" A worried expression clouded her pretty features.

"It's nothing."

"Is it too much to ask for a hug for your older brother?"

Beau flew from my arms over to Lincoln. She attacked him with the same ferocity she had me. Slowly, he wrapped her in a hug and held her tight.

My brother was mostly stoic on the exterior. I supposed he had to be to handle our father. But there was never any doubt how he felt about Beau and me.

They broke apart, and with them standing side by side, it was easy to see how similar they were despite their five-year age difference. Beau wore a royal blue dress and heels. She certainly didn't appear to have just stepped off a flight from London. And if Lincoln hadn't been playing basketball, he'd have on a suit.

Me?

I preferred jeans and a Henley.

"Where's your stuff?" I asked. "Am I going to need a U-Haul to get it to my place?"

She lifted her chin. "I only brought two bags. And I'm staying here. At least for the first part of my visit. I need my own bathroom."

"I got a new place," I said, grinning.

"Two bedrooms? Baths?"

I scratched the side of my neck. "Umm . . . not exactly."

She narrowed her gaze.

"It's a loft. You'll love it," Lincoln said.

I blinked at him in surprise. My brother was more of a Fifth Avenue penthouse kind of guy. My place would fit in his basketball court. But there was genuine appreciation on his face and he hadn't even seen it all cleaned up. He'd gone with me to take a look when I'd found it and helped me move, along with some of the guys from the station, but he'd been called away on some emergency our father had concocted.

"It's fine if you choose him over me," I said petulantly, though I didn't mean a word of it. "But at least come with me to the hospital to see an injured fireman. It would make his day."

CHAPTER ELEVEN

PEPPER

"SADIE!"

It was supper time. I was two minutes late. And that girl was barking her head off.

"You know she likes it when you reprimand her," Miss Adeline said matter-of-factly.

It was true. Completely and totally true.

The closer I got to her kennel, the faster she stomped her feet.

"All right, you," I grumbled, though I didn't mind at all.

I scooped dog food into her bowl, and she danced in anticipation of me setting it down.

"I invited Mr. October over again for dinner."

Sadie had stopped barking, so I heard Miss Adeline loud and clear . . . and nearly dropped the bowl in my hands.

Once I set it down and closed the kennel, I faced her. "Why would you do that?"

"You could use a friend. And he has the bonus of being a nice one to look at." She gave me a pointed look and continued to unstack bowls on the counter so I could fill them.

"I already have all the friends I need."

"Who? Do you have a secret companion I haven't met?"

"You," I said without looking up.

"You're going to need someone else someday. And you keep everyone at a football field distance instead of arm's length."

"I don't need anyone else." My stubborn streak reared its ugly head. "I have the dogs. And you." And I refused to think about when she would be gone from my life.

She smirked. "And Mr. October soon."

"Don't meddle, woman." I pointed at her before setting a bowl in Muffy's kennel.

"I already am."

I narrowed my gaze on her. "*When* exactly did you invite him?"

She busied herself with sliding the next bowl to me to fill. "Today."

"How?"

"I called him. That texting thing is for the birds." Miss Adeline was up with the times, but there were some things she refused to do. Texting was one of them. "People need to remember how to communicate. With their voices."

She wasn't wrong, but I wasn't in the mood for a lecture. Especially when she'd dropped a bomb that Teague was coming over for dinner.

Wait. She didn't actually say he was coming. She said she'd *invited* him. Something about that eased the tension inside me.

"What did he say?" I asked carefully as I fed Otis.

"Wouldn't you like to know?" That old woman had invented the word mischievous.

"Yes. So I know if I need to fix more food."

She put a hand on my arm. "He's coming."

Great. I'd planned on having cereal for supper. It had been a long day, and I didn't feel like spending even an hour in the kitchen.

"Hope he likes Lucky Charms," I muttered.

"He said he'd bring dinner. So if you don't want to be friends with a man who can cook, I will be." She winked.

I groaned. The funny thing was, Miss Adeline didn't have any friends either. Sure, she knew lots of people and could charm anyone.

But she wasn't exactly a social butterfly other than when she had to be for the rescue.

"It's different for me," she said as if reading my mind. "You've got a lot of life left and only having an old woman around isn't enough."

I set down the bowl I'd just picked up. "It's so much more than I deserve."

A sheen came over her eyes, but she nudged another bowl in my direction. "Don't go getting all sappy on me, girl." She grabbed a water pitcher. "Besides, if you get close with him, I benefit too. Maybe he'll bring more firemen over."

"Woman!" The word may have been a complaint, but deep down I loved her spunk.

"What? He might." She distributed the water bowls. "If you won't think of yourself, think of me."

She knew how to motivate me. Knew beyond a doubt I'd do anything for her. Did I draw the line at a parade of hot firemen? Gah. She had me thinking of them as gorgeous exteriors to look at now. The very reason I'd vehemently opposed the calendar.

"Are you going to ask your new best bud to bring over some of his friends?" I asked, not bothering to hide my sarcasm.

"Not yet. We're not close enough for that. But I'm going for an invite to the station. That way I can pick who I want to come over." Her expression was as serious as though she'd delivered a scientific fact.

"You always have a strategy."

"Always." She shoved me. "Now hurry up. Your company will be here at six thirty."

My company?

But before I had a chance to argue, Tuck flipped over his water bowl. A river ran wild. His neighbors lapped at the cold drink as fast as they could.

"Thanks for helping me clean up."

Tuck joined in, his tail waving wildly as if he were proud to take care of his own mess. The chaos was exactly what I needed to temporarily forget about Teague.

———

"I'M STARVING. And I need to walk the dogs before bed."

It was seven forty-five. Almost an hour and a half past the time he was supposed to be here. I wasn't waiting anymore.

I plunked down small bowls on the counter more aggressively than I should. Miss Adeline and I had a routine. Yeah, there were bumps in the road, but disappointment like this could be avoided.

Disappointment?

How could I be upset when I didn't want him to come over in the first place? The bran flakes tinkled against the porcelain as I poured. He'd let down Miss Adeline. *That* was why I was so irritated.

"I thought we were having Lucky Charms," she protested as I placed a bowl in front of her.

"Not tonight."

She placed a hand on mine as I reached for the milk. "I'm sorry."

"For what? You didn't do anything. Except stick your nose somewhere you shouldn't have." I flipped over my hand and squeezed back. "Are you going to stop meddling?"

"Nope."

That was what I was afraid of.

CHAPTER TWELVE

PEPPER

"WHERE'D YOU GROW UP?"

The question I dreaded most. I'd known Vivian for a while and it had never come up.

"Because I detect a hint of a drawl I've never been able to put my finger on," she continued before I could answer. "Let me guess. Georgia?"

I snickered.

"That's wrong, dang it. Mississippi?"

I wondered if we were going to do this until she'd guessed all fifty states.

I shook my head.

She let out a huff of frustration and Muffy looked back at her to see what was the matter. If only we could find a certain truck for him to do his business on again.

Oscar barked at a bird, and I grinned. "You got it right," I said gleefully to him.

Vivian elbowed me in the arm. "Miss Adeline has rubbed off on you."

I shrugged, though I hoped it was true. If I was anything like her, I'd be happy.

"Spend enough time with her and it's bound to happen." Underneath my dry tone was a fondness reserved only for the woman who'd meant so much in my life.

I was irritated with her over last night's debacle but knew good and well she wouldn't stop meddling. She did call Teague a few choice names, then turned around and told me when he apologized, I should hear him out.

He didn't owe me an apology. *She* was the one who deserved it. They'd cooked up a dinner date—not date, just . . . whatever it was. I'd had nothing to do with it.

Except some hurt feelings, a little bit of anger, and a healthy dose of disappointment. I had no right to feel any of those things. I hadn't wanted him to come over anyway.

Vivian snapped her fingers in front of my face. Oscar promptly sat. It never failed. Dogs made me smile every single day.

"Hello? Where are you?"

"On West Fourteenth. Walking the dogs."

She scowled. "Smarty pants. Are you thinking about the hot calendar fireman? Miss Adeline told me he cooked you two dinner."

That meddlesome old . . .

"No," I answered far too quickly.

She grinned. "Were too. She also told me he helped you walk all the dogs."

"You've helped me do that too. Does that mean we're taking this relationship to another level?" I tried and failed to keep the sarcasm to a minimum.

Vivian was undeterred. "Not sure Daniel would appreciate that too much. Then again . . ."

It was my turn to elbow her.

"South Carolina."

She tilted her head. "You really don't want to talk about Mr. October."

It was a toss-up which topic I'd like to discuss less. But yes, I definitely didn't want to even think about him.

"There's nothing to talk about." I waved my hand dismissively.

Mischief was written all over her face. "Well, now I do. Geography is kind of boring anyway."

"How are things going for the fundraiser?"

She burst out laughing. "I had no idea you'd go to such great lengths to get out of talking about a man."

"You and Miss Adeline are quite the tag team," I grumbled. "Two against one isn't fair."

"Aww. Don't be like that."

We smiled at each other. Vivian wasn't afraid to say what she thought but was never overpowering. I admired that about her.

Otis yanked on the leash, catching me off guard. I stumbled forward as he took off at a sprint down the sidewalk.

"Otis! Stop!" He was a greyhound. I was an out-of-shape woman in my mid-thirties. The math was not in my favor.

Sadie didn't feel like joining in, so I had one dog racing in front of me and one standing in place behind me. My arms stretched as far apart as they could.

"Pepper!" Vivian yelled helplessly.

And then Otis stopped and sat.

At the feet . . . of the dog treat guy, who was loading boxes into his van.

Garrison sold gourmet treats at his shop around the corner and always had something for my pups. He was most likely Otis's favorite person on the planet and would do anything for the man.

I panted as if I'd just run a half marathon. Sadie sighed as she caught up, annoyed she'd had to trot. Her tail wagged when she saw Garrison.

"Please tell me you have something for him," I pleaded. "I don't think I could do another sprint all the way to your shop."

He reached into his jacket pocket. Otis sat up straighter. "No more sprints for you today."

I nearly sagged in relief. Sadie reached out her long leg and pawed at Garrison. That girl. She didn't have the best manners.

He didn't seem to mind. "Otis, you get yours first. Even though you nearly pulled Mom's arm out of socket."

Otis wagged his tail at that. When Garrison offered him a biscuit, he gently took it from his hand.

"Hello, Oscar," he continued, offering the dog a treat. Oscar smacked happily.

Sadie barked, obviously none too happy at being overlooked.

"Muffy." Garrison pointed to the sidewalk, and he sat obediently. "Good boy."

I was pretty impressed myself. It was a fifty-fifty shot if any of the dogs would do as told. I wasn't the best trainer.

Sadie barked again, louder this time, as if Garrison or half of Manhattan hadn't heard her before.

"You are so much trouble, young lady." But the fondness was in his eyes as he offered her a treat.

She nearly took his fingers off when she snatched it away. There was no point in apologizing when she'd do the same thing again and again. Sadie was the way she was. And I loved her for it.

I looked around at the group of dogs.

I loved all of them. Maybe more than I should.

"Will you cater the fundraiser?" Vivian blurted. "I don't know why I didn't think of it earlier."

"Umm . . . sure. The dog treats are edible for humans, but I'm not sure your guests will be into that," Garrison said.

I bit my lip so as not to laugh. Miss Adeline was going to love this story.

Vivian turned bright red. "I meant for the dogs."

And then they wore matching shades of crimson on their cheeks.

"Oh. Ohh. Of course. Let me know the date and consider it done," he said.

"Thank you." It wasn't enough, but I appreciated all he did for the Grey Paws family.

"No need. But you're welcome." He brightened. "Have this." He rummaged around in his van until he found the box he was looking for. "It's a new cookie. No sugar or gluten. Just puppy-healthy ingredients."

I tucked the box under my arm. "The dogs will love these."

"Let me know what they think. They're my test market." He grinned and discreetly snuck Otis another treat.

"Have you considered getting another dog?" Vivian asked as she watched the two of them intently.

He looked at Otis apologetically. "I'm not ready yet." His voice held the quiet pain of loss that I understood all too well. "I-I should be on my way." He motioned toward the van.

"I'll drop by in a few days," she said.

"Anytime."

It took an effort to get Otis to resume our walk, and when we did, he headed back toward the rescue. Sadie seemed to like the idea, joining him. We all followed at a leisurely pace.

"We're going to get them all homes. At the event," Vivian said with determination.

That feeling I had when I left the dogs at the track back in Virginia filled me. Like someone had tied a rope around my chest . . . and then stepped on it.

I wanted these dogs to have the homes they deserved. That was what Miss Adeline and I did. But because we were so small—or maybe I just got too attached—every single dog that came through our doors was more than someone else to be rescued.

I'd grown particularly fond of the motley crew we had now. We were a family. All of us. And the thought of Sadie not being around to announce meal time . . .

I had a serious problem. *Stop being so selfish.*

Vivian absolutely would find adopters for all of the dogs. I had no doubt. And I had a few weeks to come to terms with Grey Paws being empty . . . until the next dog needed to be rescued.

CHAPTER THIRTEEN

TEAGUE

"YOU HAVE a lot of nerve showing up here."

It wasn't the greeting from Miss Adeline I expected, but it could've been worse.

She sat behind the reception desk, phone in one hand, petting someone I couldn't see with the other.

"But I brought dinner." I held up two bags containing chili, home-made cornbread, and salad.

"A day too late," she muttered slamming down the phone. "Pepper!" she yelled. "We gotta roll."

"What did you—" Pepper halted in the doorway to the back, breathless and red-faced. Her ponytail was lopsided and there were the customary paw prints on her overalls. She looked exhausted . . . and beautiful.

Her gaze was glacial, though it didn't stay on me long. It warmed infinitely when it landed on Miss Adeline.

"That was a track in Jersey. We get four of their dogs today or—" I'd never heard that hard edge to her voice before. Even the less-than-friendly greeting had nothing on that.

"I'll make sure the van's ready." Pepper jumped into action.

"I'm coming with you," I said. It was as if the alarm at the station had gone off, and my brain shifted into automatic. "May I put this in your fridge?" I held up the bags.

A curt nod and a wave of her hand toward the stairs was all I got. I raced to their apartment and didn't think twice about barging right inside.

Even in my hurry, I noticed it was much the same as it was the last time I'd been there. Tidy, except for a few dishes in the sink, books on the table, and dog toys scattered on the floor.

The refrigerator was packed, but I managed to make room, shoving the whole bag onto a shelf.

In seconds, I slammed their front door and flew back down the stairs, ignoring the soreness in my abs.

Pepper stuffed a pack of hot dogs in a cooler with determination. "What can I grab?"

She pointed to a bag next to her without a word. Beef jerky was on top of whatever else was inside.

I gripped the handles and also picked up the cooler when she closed the lid. That earned me an annoyed look, but I ignored it and headed toward the open back door.

The dogs barked, led by Sadie who also stomped her feet. Ash stood and stuck her nose through the kennel door when I approached.

"Hey." I set the cooler down and rubbed the top of her head with a couple of fingers. "I'll be back soon."

She seemed satisfied but didn't back away from the gate. I marveled at how she recognized I'd carried her from her burning house and the attachment we seemed to have for one another.

Miss Adeline slammed the passenger door of the van. I tossed the bag and cooler in the back and turned to help Pepper with whatever else was needed. As used to moving quickly in an emergency as I was, I felt a bit out of my element. At the fire station, everyone had a duty when the alarm sounded. The tasks didn't need to be thought about. They were ingrained. Automatic.

Here, I didn't know what supplies we needed or the procedure. But these two did.

Pepper picked up a large crate by the back door.

"I'll get it." I attempted to take the awkward contraption from her but she refused, hefting it into the van.

She slammed the doors and hopped in the driver's seat. By the time I climbed into the back, she already had the van in gear.

"How does this work?" I gripped one of the crates from my position on the floor to keep from sliding around as Pepper zipped through the streets.

"Oh they usually bring the dogs out in a peaceable exchange," Miss Adeline said smartly. "They give us their dog beds and toys and bowls."

The woman had a sharp tongue, but I wasn't sure if this had to do with my missing dinner last night or because she was uptight about the rescue.

"Then this should go easy."

She glared and the slight smile on my face evaporated.

"I've been to this track before," she said, turning her attention to Pepper. "It's been a long time, but I doubt it's changed much."

"Back entrance?" Pepper was all business, her gaze laser-focused out the windshield.

"No. If it's the same as it used to be, the kennels are to the left once we get in the gate." She tapped on the screen of a smartphone I wouldn't have expected her to have. "They have races starting at six, so we should be able to get inside easily enough."

"If we can't?"

"We do like always and improvise."

These two sounded like they were preparing for a battle. If someone had called to ask them to come get the dogs, why wouldn't they turn them over easily? Apparently I had a lot to learn about rescues.

"What do you want me to do?" With an emergency, every situation was different, but things went better when you worked as a team. Today, I'd be on the receiving end of the orders, but I liked this captain much better than my normal one.

"Stay in the van," Pepper snapped.

"No way." I couldn't sit by and do nothing. She shouldn't expect that of me.

She flicked her cool gaze to me in the rearview mirror. I liked that she was in command and no nonsense, especially when it came to the dogs.

"You can get the crates open and ready," she relented.

I scowled. I could do more than that. What if the situation was dangerous inside the kennels? I should be there to look out for them.

They've done this a million times without you.

Didn't matter. I was on this rescue. I'd do my part . . . whatever that was.

AFTER WHAT SEEMED like only minutes, the entrance to the track came into view.

Miss Adeline straightened.

Pepper gripped the wheel harder.

And my blood pumped a little faster through my veins.

The arch over the entry was rusted. What few parking lot lights remained weren't straight up any longer. The paint was faded on them and most of them didn't have working bulbs.

If this place was in this kind of disrepair, what did it say about the care of the dogs?

Anger for the animals bubbled to the surface.

Miss Adeline turned and pointed at me. "Don't say anything. We go in. We get the dogs. We get out."

I nodded once, but she was already directing Pepper toward where she believed the kennels to be.

There were few cars in the parking lot. I wasn't sure if that was a good thing or a bad thing. Would we need witnesses?

Pepper wheeled the van to a building that looked like it could use a coat of paint.

"This is it," Miss Adeline said. She had her door open before we stopped.

"Get the crates open and keep guard." Pepper gave me a pointed look. "Stay put."

She grabbed several leads and hooked them over her neck.

I didn't like this. I didn't like being left outside. Not when I was meant to be doing *something*.

The dome light in the van provided the only source of light and it wasn't much. There was a fixture by the door to the kennels that kept flickering like it could go out any second.

I tensed my shoulders. The trees rustled in the cold wind, but there was no other noise.

It was too quiet. With every snap of a branch I jerked to hear where the sound came from like I was in some sort of bad horror movie. It was the unexpected I didn't care for. I preferred to know what was coming, or at least the possibilities.

Woof. Woof. Woof.

Crazed barking ensued and seconds later, Pepper burst out the door with four dogs. How had she gotten a leash on all of them that quickly?

I rushed toward her, but she shook her head. "Help me get them in. I have to go back."

"I thought we were getting four?"

She shoved the leads in my hand and jogged back toward the building. I bent to heft one of the dogs into the van but realized I had three others to contend with. They were sniffing and jerking—and strong.

Pepper would've probably already had them in the van.

I wrapped the leads around my hand and just went for it. The dog I picked up was the most active. He wiggled in my arms so violently I thought he might escape.

"Hey now. It's okay. We're here to help."

He didn't seem to understand. In fact, he fought harder. I hoped I wasn't hurting him and hated to stress the poor guy out.

The more he resisted the more anxious the others became. But I got him inside a crate and secured the door.

Pepper appeared again with another three dogs. I worked faster to get the next one in the van. She took the remaining leashes out of my hand, making it easier to get them inside.

"Load them through the side door," she said when we'd run out of crates.

She was calm. In command.

Where is Miss Adeline?

The barking had settled and the night had become suspiciously quiet again. Pepper disappeared into the building once more.

I guided the last dog around to the side door. He—or was he a she —put his paws on the side step as if he knew he was headed for safety.

But he couldn't jump up.

As I gave him a boost, I got a good look at him in the light. His ribs were visible. He had bumps on his skin. And he appeared as though he could break with the slightest touch.

Gently, I put him in the van and patted a blanket on the floor. He lay down on it immediately.

Miss Adeline emerged with two more dogs. She moved in a light-ning clip, especially for a person her age.

"Hey!"

She didn't look up when someone shouted, a woman on a mission.

A shadowy figure hurried toward us. Miss Adeline continued to ignore him. I helped her load the dogs in the van and opened the passenger door so she could easily get inside.

"Those aren't the dogs you're supposed to take," he said breath-lessly when he reached us.

"Tell that to the sheriff when I report you for cruelty to animals." She muscled in front of me instead of climbing in the van.

"Those dogs are spoiled," he shouted as he took a step closer. "Give them back or you'll be talking to the cops for stealing."

She snorted. "No one has seen your ribs in fifteen years from the looks of it. The same can't be said for the greys we found."

"I have races to run tonight." He moved toward the open van doors.

I put up a hand without touching his chest. "You don't want to do that."

He looked up at me, appearing to assess just how great a threat I was. "Give me back the dogs and we won't have a problem." His tone had lost a bit of its bravado.

"We already have a problem," Miss Adeline snapped. "I have malnourished dogs with some in obvious need of medical care."

Pepper burst out of the building with four more dogs. Holy crap.

"You can't have those dogs. They're running a race in an hour."

What? Three of them could barely walk. They seemed to have summoned all their strength to make it this far.

One collapsed at my feet as if he knew he'd made it to safety.

I scooped him up and settled him next to the others, then repeated with the remaining dogs.

"This it?" I asked gruffly.

Pepper nodded as the man made a grab for the leads still in her hands.

"Do *not* touch them."

He froze at my command. "You can't take my dogs."

"You don't have dogs anymore." Miss Adeline climbed in the van and slammed the door.

Pepper tossed the leashes in the back.

"Get in."

She flashed me a look to kill but didn't argue. I closed her inside and the dome light went out.

"You can't do this." The man made no move.

"You shouldn't have done what you did." I shouldered past him.

"I called her to come get some of them," he cried.

"So you got one thing right. Don't make another mistake."

I jogged around the front of the van.

Pepper screamed.

I reversed course to find the man had opened the side door.

Dogs barked viciously.

The man fought for the leashes in her hand. She kicked her legs wildly, landing a couple blows to his stomach.

"Leave them alone," she screamed.

I yanked on his shoulders and tossed him to the ground.

"Ahh!" He landed flat on his back.

I put a boot on his chest. "I said don't make another mistake." I pressed a little harder to emphasize the point before I removed my foot.

"Lock it." I closed the van doors again and sprinted around to the driver's side.

Thank God Pepper had never turned off the ignition. I threw it into gear and slammed on the gas.

No one said a word until we were off the track property.

"Is this what all rescues are like?" I asked.

"No," Miss Adeline said. "We don't usually get caught."

CHAPTER FOURTEEN

PEPPER

THIRTEEN.

What were we going to do with thirteen more dogs? We were already out of kennels. And our donation funds were nearly dry. After the vet bill from Dr. Lyons came in, the coffers would be depleted.

When I'd gone in that track kennel and seen the conditions, I'd nearly been paralyzed. It didn't matter how many ugly situations I'd seen. It never got any easier.

But we'd rescued them.

They were safe now. And thankfully most of them just needed to put some weight on, although a couple were dangerously underweight and one had a fractured leg.

Dr. Lyons had kept them for observation.

There was a sea of greyhounds at my feet as I filled water bowls.

It was nearly ten o'clock. I still had to walk the other dogs before bed. And I had to figure out where our new friends would sleep. We didn't have enough crates. Maybe they'd have to come upstairs.

"We'll be fine." Miss Adeline patted my shoulder. "We always are."

"I know." And I did. But I was exhausted.

A big part of my stress was Teague. I was grateful he'd been there for the rescue. Why though? He'd stood us up yesterday. And now, he wouldn't leave.

Whatever Miss Adeline or I commanded him to do, he did. He'd kept his cool at the track. He'd taken up for us.

Because of that, I'd already forgiven him for the missed dinner. I just hadn't forgotten it yet.

He grabbed a couple leads. "Is there an order to who goes out first?"

Sadie barked like she understood the question and was responding "Me. Me. Me."

He grinned and opened her kennel door. She bolted out to inspect our new friends. Her nose worked overtime as she sniffed each one in welcome.

When she was finished, she rubbed against Teague's legs and looked at him innocently. I rolled my eyes. She was so much trouble.

He rubbed her head. "Ready to go out?"

That tender voice he used with the dogs got me every single time. I'd heard him reassure the greys we'd rescued. He'd been good—no, great—with them. I wasn't sure how I felt about that. Only that it made my heart beat a little faster. He was a good man.

Sadie stamped her feet and impatiently waited for him to loop her neck with the leash. Once he had, she marched over to Ash's kennel and nudged the door with her nose.

Ash got to her feet, her tail going a million miles a minute. She didn't react like that for anyone except Teague. But it made sense. He'd saved her.

"This who you want as your walking partner?" he asked Sadie, who barked and nudged the door again. "Okay."

Sadie was unusually calm as he leashed Ash.

"You don't have to do this," I said instead of the thank you I'd meant to come out.

"I want to."

We stared at one another for a moment. His brown eyes were piercing, like they could cut straight through to my soul. I couldn't look away. I couldn't get away from what that look stirred inside me. It was indescribable because I'd never felt *that*. Whatever it was.

Sadie tugged on the leash, having had enough of standing around, and went for the back door. They disappeared, and I stood staring after them.

"He's good with them."

I jumped and put my hand over my heart. "Why'd you sneak up on me?"

"A bulldozer could have, the way you were staring." That woman. I hated it when she was right.

"After I bathe them, we should let them sleep upstairs."

She smirked as I ignored her comment. "Agreed. I'll gather up some blankets, but tomorrow we'll get them beds. I'll call in a favor." She surveyed the space. "We don't have room for more kennels, but we need to think of something more permanent. We're going to have a full house for a while."

I looked at all the dogs scattered on the floor. There were so many it was hard to walk without stepping on one.

"Will the track give us any trouble?" A niggle of worry wound its way through me. I didn't particularly like taking more dogs than we were called about, but there was no way on earth I'd have left any of them behind.

This wasn't the first time it had happened. And it wouldn't be the last.

She waved her hand in the air dismissively. "Nah." Then she placed that hand on her hip and looked around. "So baths for all the new pups up next?"

It was nearly eleven o'clock. But it needed to be done.

"Yeah. And looks like you're going to have a lot of bedfellows tonight." I grinned, but it felt tired.

"I better see if I can find extra blankets. Once I get everything ready, I'll be back down to help."

I set a water bowl in front of one our new family members. He greedily lapped it up.

"I've got it. You can take the early shift tomorrow."

She scowled. "I always get the early shift. It's like you think old people are up before the sun."

"You *are* up before the sun." I bit my lip to keep from laughing.

She shook her finger at me. "I can't wait until you're my age."

"Me neither. Then I can say what I want, when I want, without worrying what anybody else thinks."

She stroked the closest dog. "You should do that anyway."

————

"YOU GIVE the term 'piss like a race horse' new meaning."

I nearly dropped the shampoo bottle at Teague's words.

"Except you're a dog, not a horse." He scratched behind Muffy's ears.

I always found it fascinating how quickly people started talking to dogs in real speak. Like we expected them to answer. They did seem to understand a lot more than they received credit for.

Red crept up Teague's neck when he caught me eavesdropping. "Think that's everyone. No cold walk for you tonight."

If he hadn't been here, this would've been an even longer night. I'd only bathed three dogs so far and now that they had figured out what was happening, they were becoming a bit uncooperative.

"Thanks." I'd never been great at expressing my feelings. That word wasn't enough for how overwhelmed with gratitude I was for all he'd done, but it was the best I could come up with.

He set Muffy free, who ran directly over to me.

"You want a bath?"

He sat at my feet, that tail dragging across like a windshield wiper at full speed.

"We gotta get these guys clean first. How about tomorrow?" I bent to kiss the top of his head and his tail wagged faster. He put a paw on my thigh. I shook it. "Deal. For now, you can supervise."

This seemed to make him inordinately happy. He inspected the dog in the wash station as if checking my work.

I toweled off the wet dog and let him go before I found the next willing participant. She hesitantly allowed me to lead her to the wash station, her legs shaking violently.

I scratched behind her ears and Muffy licked her foot as if comforting her. He was such a gentle soul.

"It's okay, sweet girl. This is going to feel good." I turned on the water and let her get used to it running out of the nozzle.

Warmth hit my back. I jumped.

"You rinse, I'll scrub?" The deep voice in my ear sent a tremor through me.

"I've got it," I argued half-heartedly. "I'm sure you have things to do. And it's late."

Excuse after excuse fell out of my mouth. I wasn't sure if I wanted him to take the out or stay.

He swiped the shampoo bottle and squirted some in his palm.

Teague was staying.

And I was relieved.

I rinsed the dog, and he began lathering her up.

"Feels good, doesn't it?" He spoke in a soothing tone as he massaged the soap onto her sides. "Wanna know a secret? I wasn't much for baths either when I was young." Her ear perked up, like she understood they'd found common ground. I found myself leaning closer too . . . curious. "My mom would put me in a plastic pool because I liked that and I'd scream if she put me anywhere close to a tub."

The vivid image of him as a child popped into my head. I couldn't picture him being afraid of anything but could easily see him in one of those pools.

"I was a big pain in the behind." He continued lathering, and she wasn't shaking nearly as much as she had been before.

"Was?" The word popped out of my mouth without thought, and I wanted to kick myself. He'd been telling interesting stories and I'd likely ruined the moment.

He arched a brow at the same time a corner of his mouth lifted. "Yeah. *Was.*"

The dog licked him in the face, and he grinned.

"They all like you," I said quietly.

"What about you?"

I shrugged. "Not much."

His smile broadened. He should have his own calendar, not just one month. But I wouldn't admit that to Miss Adeline. Or to him.

"I can work with a little."

He took another lick to the face. "You are an affectionate thing."

A shrill bark I didn't recognize echoed through the space. We both turned to find Ash on her feet, nose pressed through the kennel door.

"I think she might be jealous." The girl had been through so much. I was thrilled to see her coming out of her shell, telling us how she felt.

"You're still my girl," he called as he flicked his chin at her.

He couldn't be this person. It was a lot easier when I thought he was a jerk. The more I got to know him, the more I chalked up our first encounter to a bad day.

He was all tough on the exterior. While we were at the track and things got crazy, he didn't even flinch. He kept his cool. Defended us.

But inside . . . he had a tender heart.

"Hey! You sprayed me."

I looked down. The nozzle was pointed at him instead of the dog. "Oops."

"I'll oops you." He put a glob of suds on my nose.

I wiped them away with the back of my hand . . . then squirted more water at his chest.

"This your way of trying to get my clothes off?" He smirked.

I became so hot with embarrassment I almost sprayed myself to cool off. "Definitely not."

But it wasn't a bad idea.

I stiffened and focused back on the task at hand. Washing the dog. *Not* spraying Teague down.

I felt his eyes on me as I rinsed the same spot on her but pretended not to notice.

Eventually, he returned to his work. "I thought it was pretty dang creative myself."

Heat rushed through me again. "Not every woman wants you naked," I snapped.

"Aww, now you're just hurting my fragile ego."

I snorted. "You're not fragile."

"I'm sensitive."

I cut my eyes over to him and he batted his lashes innocently. "I should spray you again."

"Then it'll only be fair if I get to spray you back," he warned.

"Hmph."

After a final rinse, I turned off the water and toweled the dog off. She wasn't shaking anymore, so that was a win.

Teague gently set her on the floor and she lay beside him. He scooped another dog up as if he weighed nothing.

This one tucked his tail as if he'd accepted his fate. The dreaded bath.

"I'm sorry," Teague said as he massaged shampoo into the dog's skin. "About yesterday. My sister arrived into town early and she wanted to go see Cassano."

"It's fine. You have no obligation to us." But my tone said otherwise. That it wasn't fine. And I didn't want him to know he'd hurt my feelings. Actually, I didn't want him to have the power to hurt my feelings. Maybe that was what bothered me most.

"He was injured in the fire where I found Ash. Almost died." Teague paused scrubbing as if trying to collect himself. "It could've been me." He resumed shampooing. "Maybe it should've been."

The last part was spoken so quietly I almost missed it. Survivor's guilt. It was obvious he was struggling with it.

"I'm sure your visit meant a lot to him."

He shrugged. "Or my sister's did."

The playfulness was back, and I was relieved. I didn't like to see him upset, though I wasn't exactly sure why it mattered.

"Where does your sister live?" Curiosity got the better of me, even as my brain screamed at me not to learn any more about this man or I'd be in trouble.

"London."

Oh. Wow. I'd been thinking Rhode Island or somewhere stateside.

"Are you close?" No. No. No. *Stop asking personal questions.*

The way his features brightened told me everything I needed to know.

"Yeah. She's a giant pain in the behind, but I wish she'd move back." He rinsed the suds from his hands. "She annoys our brother more than she does me."

"You have a brother?"

Apparently I'd gone all in on investigating every nook and cranny about him.

"An older one. Who also is a pain in the ass."

"Sounds like it runs in the family."

He snorted. "I guess it does."

WE FINISHED BATHING the last dog and all the others were sound asleep.

"What do you need?" Teague asked, just above a whisper.

I looked around, not even sure where to start.

"Food. Beds. Bowls." I threw my hands up. "Everything."

He slid an arm around my shoulders and pulled me into a hug. I dropped my forehead against his chest and breathed in his soothing scent. He rested his chin on top of my head and held me tighter.

Eventually, I gave in and put my arms around his waist.

I needed this.

A moment of reprieve. Where someone would make me feel like it was all going to be okay even if it wasn't.

I closed my eyes.

He rubbed a strong, comforting hand up and down my back. I held on.

"We'll get through it."

I wanted to tell him to save promises he couldn't keep.

We skated by on sporadic donations and did the best we could with what we had. Somehow we managed to stretch and keep going. But there was never enough money.

Because there were always more dogs to be rescued.

We were about to the point that if we received a call today, we'd have to say no. But we wouldn't.

We *couldn't*.

No matter how hard it got, we always figured it out.

Miss Adeline and me. No one else.

Yet I couldn't seem to tear myself out of his embrace.

His warmth brought a comfort I rarely, if ever, felt from another human. The dogs gave me peace. They didn't care if my clothes were stained or I didn't brush my hair or if I ate too much cake.

They loved me at my worst just as much as they did at my best.

Teague had gotten a glimpse at the not so glamorous side of my life. Instead of making excuses to leave, he'd jumped right into the chaos.

And I wasn't sure what to do with that.

I yawned and sank further into him.

"Is that my cue to go?" His voice had a tease that brought a weary smile to my face.

"I think so." Reluctantly, I lifted my head and was almost certain disappointment was etched on his features. "I appreciate . . . everything."

I squeezed him one last time before I dropped my arms. He inched closer. I held my breath. He'd already mesmerized me tonight. His care for the dogs. The safety they'd felt in his arms. I'd wanted that. And now, he was giving me that same safety, and I appreciated it more than I'd be able to communicate. I'd say he smelled great, but he truly smelled like dog. Clean dog, but still. And of course, I even loved that.

But now, as he drew closer, I wondered.

Is he going to kiss me?

I froze, stuck between the desire to feel his lips on me and scared of what would happen if he did.

He was so close, the heat as he exhaled hit my skin. The moment of impact was imminent. And I didn't know what I'd do.

Just before his mouth reached my forehead, he stopped.

Disappointment and relief sailed through me.

He cleared his throat as if coming out of the same fog I was in.

"I'm gonna head out." He pointed with his thumb over his shoulder. "Unless you need me."

The statement was too loaded for me to process. I wasn't generally good with men, I knew that. I wasn't exactly shy but more introverted. I'd never thought myself particularly . . . interesting. As if they would bore easily of me. And so this moment with Teague was going to be one of those times I chalked my answer and his departure to my reticence. Again.

"Umm . . . no. I'll let you out."

We tiptoed to the front door. Only a few dogs raised their heads when we moved.

I twisted the lock and pushed the door open. He hesitated but eventually walked through, flicking his chin at me as he passed.

Once he was gone and the door was secure, I sagged against it.

What a day. *What* was happening?

Too exhausted to think about it, I shoved off the door and quietly approached the now sleeping pile of dogs.

I found an empty spot among them, lay down, and crashed.

CHAPTER FIFTEEN

TEAGUE

"YOU WANT TO GO SHOPPING?"

My sister looked at me as if I'd grown another head.

"Yeah." I said the word as if I lived for shopping.

She knew me all too well. How many times had she begged me to tag along with her to Saks Fifth Avenue, or hell, even to a street market?

A dark brow rose, but she didn't press me on my change of heart. "Let me grab my purse. Will you pour my smoothie into a to-go mug?"

She disappeared before I could answer. I rifled around in our brother's kitchen cabinets until I found an insulated mug. It was a little after nine, but I guessed he'd been gone for hours.

Our sister was in town from the other side of the world for a short time. We hadn't seen her in . . . I couldn't remember. Too long. Instead of spending time together, Lincoln went to work.

She sauntered back into the room and slung her purse on the island before she shrugged on her coat.

"How'd you get out of going to the office?" I poured her smoothie into the mug and rinsed out the blender.

"Jet lag." She winked.

I put my hand over my heart and staggered backward. "I can't believe you of all people."

My brother was a straight-up workaholic; my sister was a close second. But at least she knew how to let loose.

She laughed and wrapped a scarf around her neck. "Let's just not get caught out and about, okay?"

"You'd definitely better not be seen hanging around with me." The familiar bitterness crept in that I couldn't seem to let go.

Beau placed her delicate hand on my arm. "I don't give a damn what he thinks." She snatched the mug out of my grip. "Let's get out of here before you change your mind."

She didn't like to dwell on the negative. Even as a kid, she'd been like that. And I didn't want to let my father ruin our day together either. He'd done enough.

"I'm in this for the long haul today."

She looked at me strangely again before she shook her head. "Who are you and what have you done with my brother?"

AN HOUR LATER, I questioned my sanity at asking my sister to go shopping. Why I thought we'd be able to go in, get what we needed, and get out was beyond me. I should've known better.

This was the third store we'd been in.

"Will this padding give a greyhound enough support?"

The kid working at the pet supply shop blinked at Beau. He'd been dazed since he laid eyes on my sister, but now he looked as if she'd given him the final *Jeopardy!* answer and he had no idea what the question was.

Beau tapped her foot and squeezed the dog bed again before she made a disgruntled noise.

"They don't have what we want." She looped her arm through mine and led me to the entrance.

Once we were outside she hustled with determined steps to who knew where.

"I appreciate your enthusiasm," I started, my long strides barely a match for hers. "And I want them to have the best too, but they need something today."

She glared. "I haven't lived here in a long time. It's taken me a minute to get warmed up, but I remember a store a friend used to love."

"Why would a friend recommend a pet store to you? You've never had any pets," I said as she dragged me down the sidewalk. "Can we slow down?"

"You're the one who said we're in a hurry." If anything, she walked even faster. "And I had to buy gifts for people with pets." No one could put me in my place like my sister.

"I thought we could just do one store and get this done," I muttered. It wasn't only the shopping I wasn't crazy about. There were a lot of dogs with no beds, bowls, and food who needed them yesterday.

"If you'd have given me some notice, I could've done prep work."

"For shopping?"

"It's no different than basketball. When there's a game plan, there's greater success."

I stared at her. Was she serious? It didn't take but a second for me to see that yes. Yes, she was.

"Don't worry. We're about to make a half-court shot." She grinned.

I got nervous.

"We should've brought my truck."

Her smile grew wider. "And some of your fire station buddies."

I snorted and tried to smile back, though the mention of them was like a punch in the gut. It had been two days since I'd seen or spoken to any of them except Cassano. I missed my job.

"Hey." Beau punched me in the arm. "You'll be back to work before you know it."

Maybe I wasn't like her and Lincoln, driven and cut out for corporate life. But I was dedicated to my job. It fulfilled me.

If it hadn't been for Pepper and the dogs, I'd have been floundering the past few days.

Even I could admit I needed the time off to heal. Time I wouldn't have taken if not for the suspension. Ugh. The bullshit suspension.

"Are you going to punch something?"

I blinked at Beau and realized my fist was balled tight.

"Not today." I tilted my head. "At least it's not in the plan."

She relaxed her shoulders. "After you see the damage I do in this store, you might add it in."

I stopped. She stretched between where she held on to me with one hand and the door handle in the other.

I pulled her into a hug. She released the door handle and gave in.

"I'm glad you're home." I squeezed her.

She held me tight. "This isn't ho—"

"This will always be your home."

After a minute, she whispered so low I barely heard it. "I'm glad to be home too."

CHAPTER SIXTEEN

PEPPER

"WHEN YOU GET TOWED, I don't want to hear a single complaint."

I paused brushing Muffy's teeth and craned my neck at the sound of the female voice coming from the lobby.

"I'm not getting towed." Now that voice I recognized. "Unless you keep talking more than you're unloading."

A little buzz started in my ears. I'd loosened my grip on Muffy, who happily escaped and jetted toward the front of the building.

Slowly, I stood. What was *he* doing here? And unloading.

I set the toothbrush down and followed Muffy. When I moved, a whole herd of dogs followed me.

"Oh wow." The beautiful woman who stood next to Teague looked at the mass of greyhounds surrounding me with bulging eyes. "I don't think we brought enough."

"Special delivery." He held up a big box.

"Teague?"

I looked between him and the woman, distracted by their similar features. Her hair was darker, but their eyes were the same brown shade. They both had high cheekbones and olive skin. And she was nearly as tall as him. When I saw her heeled boots, I realized why.

She elbowed him in the side. "She's talking to you," she whisper-hissed.

His cheeks turned pink. "Hey."

"Hi." Oh my gosh. Were we really standing here like two teenagers with a crush? Wait. He wouldn't have a crush, but I was sure acting like I did. I cleared my throat. "What's all this?"

"A few things for these special guys." The woman set her box on the floor and squatted down.

Some of the dogs immediately went to her. She looked expensive but didn't seem to mind getting a little hair on her coat.

"Did you say something about getting towed?" I asked when I found my voice.

"He double-parked." She motioned outside where Teague's truck was definitely illegally parked.

"Want to pull in the alley?" I offered.

"Probably not a bad idea." He placed his box on the floor. Muffy immediately went to sniff it.

"It was when I suggested it," she said, exasperated.

He jogged out the door without engaging. The truck rumbled to life and disappeared.

"I'm Beau." She offered her hand but didn't stand, still interested in the dogs. "I see now why this was so urgent for him." She smirked as she took me in.

"Pepper." Suddenly, I became aware of how unkempt I was compared to her. I was wearing the same thing I'd worn yesterday. I'd overslept. The dogs couldn't wait. I'd gotten busy and never had time to shower.

I touched a loose strand of my stringy hair. I hoped Teague didn't notice.

Beau sat on the floor and a few more dogs swarmed her. She laughed and gave every one of them attention.

"Oh." I rocked onto the balls of my feet. "I should go open the back door."

"It won't hurt him to stand out in the cold." She waved her hand and grinned wickedly.

The woman was magnetic.

What if they weren't related?

Frantically, I searched her finger for a ring, but she moved too fast as she petted the dogs for me to catch a glimpse.

Knock. Knock. Knock.

Woof. Woof. Woof. Woof. Woof.

"Too late." I hustled to the back door along with all the dogs who weren't occupied by Beau.

Sadie and Ash put their paws on their kennel doors as I passed.

I opened it a crack and peeked through.

"It's me." Teague leaned closer.

"I know. But I just realized if we open the door all these loose hooligans will sprint outside." I held up my finger. "Give me a sec."

I moved back to the front room and they all followed.

Beau blinked at me in confusion. "What happened?"

"Mind keeping them occupied for a minute?" I slipped into the back room again and closed the door.

Ash dug at her kennel, desperate to get out. Because she knew Teague was near.

I propped open the door and gasped.

The entire bed of his truck was filled. He opened the passenger side doors and the backseat was stuffed to the brim too.

"Teague?" I put my hand to my chest and stared.

"This will go a little faster if you help, but I don't blame you if you'd rather watch me in action." He flexed his bicep, which I couldn't see under his jacket but knew full well how powerful it was.

I heard a strange sound echoing off the brick of the building and the metal of his truck.

It was me. Laughing.

"Give me a box, Mr. October."

"You start with the stuff in the cab and I'll grab this?" He waited for my approval, and I found I appreciated that.

I nodded and picked up as many bags as I could carry.

"Let me unload this and I'll give you all the belly rubs you want."

I nearly tripped at the sound of Teague talking to the dogs. It got me every single time.

I dropped the bags on what little empty counter space I could find, trying to keep the floor open for him. The back room was tidy but already crowded with kennels and supplies.

I resumed unloading. By the time I'd cleared the truck cab, Teague only had a few boxes left in the bed. They were unmarked other than an LLC name and a bunch of numbers on the side. I still had no idea what was in them.

I climbed into the back of the truck and slid the remaining boxes toward the lowered tailgate. When I'd finished, I hopped off and grabbed one.

Teague lifted his chin as we passed one another.

Teamwork.

He tugged on what was left of my ponytail and grinned like a kid.

I grinned back.

"IS it okay if I leave the truck parked here?" He dropped the last box on the stack of others.

"As long as you're not blocking the alley it should be fine."

He clicked the locks and closed the back door.

I stared at the mountain of boxes.

Scratching of paws on the metal door separating the front and back rooms grew more fervent. It opened, but only a fraction because it ran into a wall of boxes.

Miss Adeline poked her head through. "What in the world?"

"I've been asking the same thing," I called.

A dog slipped through the open door and barreled over and around the cardboard. An avalanche of boxes and dogs ensued until the neat rows Teague had stacked were utter chaos.

Ash barked and pounded on her kennel, her patience officially spent. Teague opened the latch and she rocketed between his legs, her whole body wiggling in happiness. He bent to stroke her head and spoke to her in a hushed tone.

With the door now wide open, Miss Adeline stood with her hand on her hip.

Beau was right behind her. "Anybody know where a knife is?"

"Thank goodness that and some scissors are in the desk behind you," Miss Adeline said. "We're going to have to cut our way out of this mess."

"If we break the boxes down, I'll haul them to the recycling center when we're finished."

Teague's thoughtfulness continually caught me off guard. Maybe I always saw the worst in people. It was what life had thrown at me. But maybe I'd been wrong.

"Thanks." I opened a drawer in the long set of cabinets that lined one wall. "Need a knife?"

I extended it to him and grabbed a pair of scissors. He took it and waited for me to open the first box.

Miss Adeline beat everyone. She pulled out a giant dog bed almost as big as she was. "Is this one for me?"

"We can have it monogrammed with your name if you want," Beau said.

Miss Adeline pointed an old, crooked finger at her. "Sassy pants."

Beau nodded. "I've been called worse."

I surveyed the mess and did a quick calculation. There weren't just beds for the new dogs but for everyone here.

"You didn't have to do this," I whispered, trying with all my might not to cry.

"You said you needed beds." He studied me, almost as if trying to see if I was pleased.

I looked away or I would cry. Now wasn't the time. Especially with his sister here. She was so put together, and I was just a mess. And un-showered, gross, but appreciative mess.

"Thank you." Those were the only words I could get out.

"Are we going to open these or leave them piled up?"

Before I could answer, Muffy attacked one of the boxes, ripping it open with his teeth. He stood proudly with little pieces of cardboard all around him.

"I guess we're opening them."

CHAPTER SEVENTEEN

TEAGUE

"WANT TO GRAB A BITE FOR LUNCH?"

Pepper looked at her feet. "I can't. We have too many dogs to leave Miss Adeline on her own."

"Beau's with her."

She shook her head. "I can't."

We'd unpacked all the beds and scattered them throughout the shelter. Something about the word shelter didn't sit right. Miss Adeline and Pepper had created a home for the dogs. Their love and care and dedication to the animals was admirable.

"You have to be hungry. I'll run to the deli down the street and get a spread for everyone." I sounded desperate. I knew it and didn't care.

Beau was going to give me hell for this later. I didn't care about that either.

Seeing the look of awe and gratitude on Pepper's face when she saw what we'd bought, made it worth it. She'd struggled to find words for her emotions, but she didn't need them.

I liked that maybe we'd made things a little easier for her.

She loaded a stack of flattened boxes into the truck bed.

"I'm sure you have other things to do."

I leaned against the lowered tailgate. "Not really."

"Your sister is only here for a short time. *She* has things she'd rather do. And you should spend time with her." She fidgeted with the edge of a box.

"If she didn't want to be here, she wouldn't be. Besides, she's happy for the excuse to be off work."

"Gypsys, Tramps & Thieves" cranked up from my pocket. It was a reminder I hadn't been at the station in a few days. Normally, this ringtone would've been a different song by now.

Pepper arched a brow but said nothing.

"Hey, big brother." I put the phone on speaker.

"Where's Beau?" Always to the point.

"She's with me."

"I thought she had jet lag."

"She does. I'm showing her the latest therapy for that." I winked.

Pepper stared at the phone with wide eyes. My brother's abrupt style was an acquired taste.

"What therapy?"

"Come to West Seventeenth Street and you'll find out. It could help you too. You're drawn up so tight you couldn't get a speck of dust up your ass." I mouthed *sorry* to Pepper, who stifled a snicker.

"Because I'm responsible for everything," he snapped, then sighed. "I'm sorry. It's been a long day. Dad's hounding me about Beau's whereabouts."

I grimaced. I hated that so much weight was on my brother's shoulders. "He knows how to pick up a phone," I growled. Though I hoped he didn't. I wanted my baby sister as far away from that man as possible. "Why don't you just tell him to go screw himself?"

Pepper shifted uncomfortably. She'd half-turned to go back inside, but I snagged her hand and asked her with my eyes to stay. She shivered. Crap. She didn't have a coat.

I pulled her against me. She was warm and perfect, even if she was rigid.

"You know why I can't do that."

Because of Beau and me. Mostly me. If he did, my father would have more time to focus his attention on me.

"I made reservations at Keens for eight. Think the therapy session will be over by then?" The hard edge had disappeared from his tone.

"I'll have to check with the princess."

The back door burst open. "Are you two making out back here or what? We're starving."

"Who are you with?" Lincoln demanded.

I shot my sister the bird. She grinned.

"Umm . . ." I didn't know what to say. Pepper wasn't a friend per se.

"His crush," Beau shouted like we were in elementary school.

"You're dating someone?"

"No," I said quickly as if that were absurd. Pepper attempted to wriggle out of my hold. I refused to release her until she shoved at me.

When she stepped away, guilt infused my chest. I wasn't dating anyone, but my denial somehow felt like a rejection of Pepper when it wasn't meant to be that way.

"What's that address again?" he asked.

"Grey Paws," Beau chimed in. "Hurry and bring lunch for five."

"You sound better," Lincoln said sarcastically.

"If I don't eat soon, I might not be able to make it to the office tomorrow either." She put her hand to her forehead even though he couldn't see it.

Drama queen.

"Be there in an hour," he grumbled.

"An hour? I might have withered away by then."

"How do you propose I get there faster? By helicopter?" Keys jangled and what sounded like a briefcase snapping came through from the other end of the phone. Our little sister had both of us wrapped around her finger.

"That works. See you in thirty." Beau pointed down frantically and mouthed *hang up*.

I did.

Pepper's gaze darted back and forth between us as if she'd never seen such a thing, even though she and Miss Adeline had a similar dynamic. Maybe that was why I was drawn to her. Because we had things in common I'd yet to realize.

She cleared her throat. "If we're having one more for lunch, I'd better find space."

"Good luck," Beau snorted and went back inside.

I touched Pepper's shoulder. She tensed with her back to me.

"I didn't mean anything by—what I'm trying to say is . . . shit."

There was a slight tremor through her body. She covered her mouth with her hand.

I maneuvered so I was in front of her. "Are you laughing at me?"

"You were trying to say shit." She giggled, all of the stress that seemed permanently carved in her features gone.

"Yeah. Actually that's exactly what I was trying to say."

She snickered. "Seems appropriate."

"I call it like I see it." I peeled her hand away from her mouth and twined our fingers together. "And I'd still like to take you to dinner."

Her face dimmed. "I'd like that too, but I can't. This place takes all of me. There's nothing left for anything else."

Maybe. Maybe not. But she didn't say no. So this day was already so much better.

CHAPTER EIGHTEEN

PEPPER

"IS MR. FEBRUARY HERE FOR ME?"

Miss Adeline flashed a come hither look at the man who entered the lobby. He couldn't be Mr. February because he had on a three-piece suit and a cashmere overcoat, and it looked like every stitch of his clothing was tailor-made. Did tailors make underwear?

I shook my head to clear it. "I've told you, you can't greet guests that way," I whisper-hissed.

She waved me off. "They don't mind. I'm just a harmless old woman."

My brows shot up. Harmless? Not a chance.

Muffy sprinted toward him and jumped, nearly knocking the bags out of the man's hands.

"Muffy! Off!" But there was no use. He had a mind of his own. How much did dry-cleaning a suit like that cost?

The man cut his eyes down to Muffy but said nothing. There was no need for words. The flat line and scowl spoke volumes.

"I was told I could find Teague and Beau here."

I tilted my head. He was the brother. I didn't know why I hadn't imme-diately seen it. His eyes were icy compared to Beau's and Teague's. There was no warmth about him. But if what he told Teague on the phone about everything being on him was true, it made sense. When the whole load was on someone's shoulders, there wasn't time to be warm and fuzzy.

I was the living embodiment of that.

"You mean Adeline." She fluttered her lashes at him.

I didn't know whether to scream or laugh.

I rushed over to Muffy to try to get him off the expensive pants. "As long as you've got food, he's going to be glued to you."

"As long as he's got on that suit, I'm going to—"

"I thought you were into firemen," I said before she finished that sentence with whatever inappropriateness was about to come out.

"That was this morning. Now, I'm more of a men-in-suits kind of girl."

"You're breaking my heart, Miss Adeline."

I whipped my head around as Teague emerged from the back. I hoped he hadn't heard this whole conversation.

"You never bring any of your friends around. What am I supposed to do? I can't wait forever."

"I wouldn't expect you to." He smirked, his focus directed at me. At his brother's feet. Trying to get Muffy off.

"She's fine," he said with a bite that said it clearly wasn't fine.

"*He*," Teague corrected.

I paused, surprised he could tell who was who since we had so many dogs.

Muffy's nose went a mile a minute, his sniffing growing more enthusiastic. He tried to stick his head in one of the bags.

Teague's brother snapped his fingers sharply.

Muffy immediately halted.

He was a good boy but definitely selective when it came to obedience.

I looked around the room. We'd all stopped. Because Lincoln was in command.

"You're out of the office. It's okay to loosen up. We won't tell." Beau barreled over to him and grabbed the bags of food. "C'mon, ladies. If these two want to chitchat all day, let's eat."

Being around her left me feeling a little dazed and a lot in awe.

She stopped in front of the desk where Miss Adeline sat and dismantled one bag in record time.

I stood and realized Muffy hadn't followed the food. He sat at Lincoln's feet, looking up at him.

"Do you have treats in your pocket?" I asked before I thought better of it.

He scowled, though I got the impression that might be his version of nice. "No."

"Pepper, tomato soup or whatever this white looking one is?" Beau inspected the contents of the paper bowl through the lid.

"The white one. She won't touch tomato," Miss Adeline said for me.

"It's the best in the city." Teague's brother sounded offended.

I was so caught off guard that he spoke, my mouth dropped open. "More for you then."

I snapped my mouth shut. I'd fallen into the way this family spoke to one another as if I were one of them. And I wasn't.

One corner of his lips twitched.

"Where's the salad?" Beau tossed an empty bag on the floor and tore into another.

"You hung up on me before I heard a request for one."

The longer Lincoln was here, the more he seemed to thaw.

She wheeled around. "You know that without me saying."

"Been so long since you've been home, must've slipped my mind," he fired back.

"Here it is." Teague held up a large container.

Beau swiped it from him. "Miss Adeline, would you care for some salad? The house dressing is to die for."

"Pretty much everything is to die for when you're my age."

I cringed, hating when she talked like that, yet relieved she was a good sport.

Lincoln coughed and covered his mouth with his fist. Teague shot him a dirty look for laughing.

Miss Adeline shrugged. "It's true." She patted the desk beside her. "Now come sit over here, honey."

He looked a little lost but obeyed. Muffy was right on his heels.

There was enough food to cover the entire desk . . . and feed ten people. The scent of the array of dishes brought more nosy dogs in from the back. I'd let everyone out of their kennels. They were used to being free most of the day. Just because we were short on space didn't mean I'd deprive them.

Ash hung right with Teague. I glanced from them to Muffy. Why hadn't I realized how territorial these dogs were with certain humans?

And then there was Sadie. She'd bulldozed her way between Beau and the desk. Her big front paws landed on the wood and close to a sandwich.

I removed them. "There's no need to scold her. She won't listen." As if proving my point, she attempted to put her paws back. I caught them and placed them on my stomach.

Woof.

"I hear you," I said, releasing her.

"You can take your coat off," Miss Adeline purred.

"Please don't tell him he can take his suit off too." I rested my rear against the edge of the desk and picked up a bowl of soup.

"It kind of takes away the element of surprise when you blurt out my plans," she huffed.

"Ignore her."

"Seems a bit impossible," Lincoln said as he shrugged off his coat.

He was right. She was a force of nature.

Teague squeezed in beside me, our thighs touching. I resisted the urge to scoot away for his own good. If the two days of sweat buildup bothered him, he didn't show it.

Beau handed him a sandwich.

He'd scarfed down half before I'd taken two bites of soup.

"Sorry. It's a habit. If you don't eat in a hurry, the alarm might go off before you get anything down." He wiped his mouth with a napkin.

"When are you going to take my girl out on a date?"

I wanted to disappear at Miss Adeline's completely inappropriate question.

"I asked her earlier today—twice—and she shot me down," Teague replied good-naturedly.

"So you weren't lying when you said you aren't dating anyone," his brother said. "You just can't seal the deal."

I nearly spit out my soup.

"Show him how it's done, handsome."

I glared at Miss Adeline but secretly liked how she'd made a powerful man blush.

"I'm a little out of practice myself," he said quickly.

"A little? These two didn't even go to their high school prom," Beau chimed in.

I couldn't help but stare incredulously. Teague was charming and kind, not to mention good-looking. He could've taken any girl he wanted.

"I didn't go either." I shoved a bite of soup in my mouth and looked down.

He touched my knee in silent support. I wouldn't lie to myself and pretend I hadn't wanted to go, but in the grand scheme of things, it was meaningless.

"I stole my date's car and left him on the side of the road after I caught him kissing another girl." Beau continued munching on her salad as if she'd said nothing out of the ordinary.

"Why am I just now hearing this?" Lincoln growled.

Oh no. I had a feeling he'd find out who her date was and set him straight even though the guy had wronged his sister twenty years ago.

She rolled her eyes. "You don't need to know everything."

"That's what concerns me," he muttered.

"You went with . . ." Teague tapped his lips with his index finger.

"It doesn't matter," she finished. "What time do the dogs eat? I need to let the catering company know when to deliver their food every day."

What? Catering company? And I thought we were talking about the prom . . . though I was grateful to be done with the subject.

I swallowed my bite of soup. "Six and six."

"A friend of mine has a *gourmet*"—she said the word in a frou-frou voice—"dog food company. All jokes aside, it's fresh and healthy. She even makes it according to the breed."

"I'm sure it's wonderful, but we can't afford that." How I wished we could. These dogs deserved the best nutrition they could get, but specialty food was way out of budget.

Beau waved me off. "She can deliver once or twice a day. Whatever you need."

"Once," Miss Adeline said before I could decline again. "In the afternoon would be good."

I gave her a stern look, which she ignored. Come to think of it, everyone ignored me around here. And yet today? I didn't mind. Today, I felt as though I had a team of people around me who had my back. So, despite the roll of my eyes, I was incredibly humbled and thankful. Tomorrow might be a different day, but today, I'd take.

"Perfect." Beau already had out her phone, her fingers flying across the screen as she typed a text. It chimed with an incoming text almost immediately. "She'll be here at four."

Another chime sounded. Beau paled.

Teague stiffened, and Sadie nosed her leg.

"What's wrong?" Lincoln barked.

"Dad's coming."

"Where?" Teague demanded in a tone I'd never heard from him.

She looked at her phone again as if unsure she'd read the message correctly. Her gaze was wary when it lifted.

"Here."

CHAPTER NINETEEN

TEAGUE

THE SURPRISE VISITS weren't unusual.

This many in one week? Very out of the ordinary.

"Keep him away from here."

I'd spoken out of turn to my brother, once again throwing everything on him. I had no problem handling any situation on my own. When it came to our father, my default setting was to shove it onto Lincoln. Let him take care of it.

He bent his head over his phone and typed furiously. As his thumb hovered, the bells above the door jingled.

All heads snapped in that direction.

The mailman hesitated as he crossed the threshold. "Were you all waiting for me?"

A collective exhale released.

"No." Pepper moved toward him. "Do we have something good?"

"I have no idea," he said as he dug in his bag.

"Don't act like you didn't snoop."

He grinned as he handed her a stack of envelopes. "Just some bills."

"Gee. Thanks."

He waved and went on his way.

And then a shadow loomed in the doorway.

I stood in front of Pepper, Miss Adeline, the dogs, and my family as if I were some sort of shield. There was no protection from this man.

"How offensive I wasn't invited to lunch." His face was the image of disdain as he scrutinized the space.

Sadie bared her teeth at him. I liked that old girl.

Muffy sauntered over and sniffed his leg. My father kicked him.

Pepper shot off the desk and Miss Adeline was right behind her.

"Leave." She pointed toward the door. "Now."

Anyone else would've shuddered at the menace in her tone.

He laughed. "This looks like a violation to me. So many dogs. So little space."

I stalked over to him. "You heard the lady. Go."

"Now you're brave?" He sneered. "Shall I tell her what a coward you are?"

I clenched my fists and stood taller. "Only cowards make threats."

That was what he was best at. Threatening.

"Oh my prodigal son. You know I only make promises."

My gut tightened into a tangled knot. He was many things but not a liar. And eventually, he did make good on all his threats. His patience was legendary.

"If you needed to speak with me, you should've called." Beau was at my side.

"I did, my dear. Repeatedly." He ran a finger down her cheek. "And this does *not* look like jet lag."

"Dad—"

"I don't tolerate liars." He snapped his finger. "You'll come with me now."

"She's not going anywhere." Lincoln stood by Pepper.

Miss Adeline ambled in front of us. "You assaulted my dog. If you want to hang around to wait for the police, be my guest."

My father flashed her his sinister smile. "I sincerely doubt they'll be interested."

Because they were in his pocket.

"I sincerely believe they—"

"Beau. Lincoln. With me now. Or this flea motel shuts down."

"You can't do that," Pepper said.

"I can. And more importantly I will." He shoved his hands in his pockets.

He and my brother's dress style was so alike down to the cashmere overcoat. Was that by choice? Or necessity?

"The fate of this wretched place is squarely on my dear children's shoulders," he said. "What will it be?"

Beau snatched her purse off the floor, kissed Miss Adeline's cheek, and gave Pepper an apologetic look. Lincoln flicked his chin, grabbed his coat, and shoved through the front door onto the sidewalk.

"Enough with the theatrics." Our father placed a hand on Beau's shoulder. "And Teague, this includes you. I'm sure your friends wouldn't appreciate an irreversible fate because of your insolence."

Were we in medieval times? Who did he think he was? A tyrant?

He lifted a brow. Before I could walk out that door he'd have someone here taking away everything Pepper and Miss Adeline had worked for. This wasn't a flea motel. It was a sanctuary. They'd done more good in the past five seconds than he had in his entire life.

"We've done nothing to you," Pepper said. She was a fighter. And I was so proud.

"You've stolen time with my children."

She opened her mouth to argue, but she had no idea who she was dealing with.

"My truck is out back." The words were spoken as if dragged from me. I hated giving in to him, letting him win.

But if it meant protecting Pepper, Miss Adeline, and the dogs, I would.

"Excellent. We'll see you at the office."

Pepper looked at me incredulously. I was a coward when it came to this man.

I scratched behind Ash's ears and dug in my pocket for my keys.

When I finally met her gaze again, she'd gone stoic. My jaw ticked when I focused my attention on my father. "Leave. Then I will."

He appeared displeased at my ordering him around, but I wouldn't budge on this. I would not leave them on their own to deal with him.

I would pay for this. It was in his expression. But he turned on his heel and led my brother and sister down the sidewalk.

Helplessly, I stared at Pepper, begging for her to understand. The situation with him was complicated. It was one thing to defy him when I was the only one to suffer the consequences and completely another when other people I respected were involved.

"You'd better get going," she said tightly.

I squatted to give one last pet to Ash. She licked me in the face and a fresh wave of hate for my father washed over me.

I stood. Miss Adeline had her arms crossed. Pepper's gaze remained glued to the floor. A strand of her hair fell into her face. I brushed it away.

She flinched, but I couldn't help myself. I wanted to pull her into my arms, promise to fix this and that he'd never touch any of them again.

I refused to lie.

I lifted her chin so I could see her.

"I'm more sorry than you'll ever know."

CHAPTER TWENTY

TEAGUE

"SIR. You can't go back there. Sir!"

I stormed past my father's secretary toward his office. It had been sixteen years since I'd set foot in this building, but I remembered the way as if it had been sixteen minutes.

There'd been a time when I was a kid that I'd liked being here. A time when I was naïve and believed my father supported me no matter what path I chose to take in life.

No matter how hard the woman tugged on my sleeve, she couldn't stop me. I was on the warpath.

I shrugged her off and charged forward. When I shoved the heavy door to his office, it was with such force, it bounced off the wall.

He smiled at my entrance.

"I'm sorry, sir. I tried to stop him," the woman said breathlessly.

He flicked his wrist at her in a *go away* motion.

Lincoln and Beau sat in the chairs in front of his desk. There was one vacant seat in the middle. Like a prisoner resigned to my sentence, I sank into it.

The Manhattan skyline was behind my father, picture perfect from the floor-to-ceiling wall of windows. His empire.

"I don't like using these tactics to get all of you together." He leaned forward and folded his hands on the desk.

Liar.

He lived for manipulation and power.

"Then don't." I blurted the words before I thought better of it. Arguing with him was useless. He always won. Always.

"I've allowed you to gallivant for too long." He ignored my petulance and then speared his hawk-like gaze into my siblings. "You think I'm a fool who doesn't realize you've taken the burden so your brother can do as he pleases."

Beau and Lincoln were like statues on either side of me. Neither of them moved. I couldn't even hear them breathe.

"Your place is in this company. It's not a choice. Be grateful I'll allow you to reap the benefits of what I've built despite your resistance."

What *he'd* built. My brother and sister got no credit for the sacrifice and dedication they'd given. Sure, they were beyond fine financially, but what good was money if all it brought was misery.

"If you'd been faithful, you'd have a place at the top alongside your siblings. But you'll start in the mailroom and earn your way to the top."

He'd lost his mind. That was the only explanation for his behavior. I wasn't working for this company. Not now. Not ever.

"I already have a job, but thanks for the offer."

"You're suspended. One more and you'll be fired."

Ice cold raced up my spine. Why was I surprised he knew that? He floated in and out of my life as he pleased. Just when I'd get comfortable, he'd make an appearance. I was a fool to believe anything other than he knew every detail of my life.

What I'd never understood was why.

He hated me.

I planted my hands on the arms of the chair and pushed out of it. "As much fun as this family reunion has been, we're done here."

"Teague."

I'd almost reached the door. I couldn't stand the sight of him, so I kept my back to him.

"She wanted this. Don't disappoint her more than you already have."

I spun. Fire lit up my veins as I struggled to remain in place instead of throttling him. His satisfied smirk told me I'd played right into his hands. I was too angry to care.

"Why do you want me here?" It was the question I'd never been able to answer.

"This is a family business. What kind of father would I be not to desire all my children to be part of it?"

That was a canned interview answer. The words of the man who charmed the outside world to manipulate them.

I wasn't one of his sheep.

I saw right through him.

"I can't make this any clearer. I'm. Not. Working. For. You." His threats had gotten me into this office, but I had to stand firm.

I loved my career. Maybe I loved twisting the knife in my father just as much. Because when he couldn't control me, he didn't get his way. That was my only leverage against him.

He relaxed on his plush throne. "Don't be so hasty, *Son.*"

I WELCOMED the cold air when I exited the office onto Madison Avenue.

We'd had this conversation more times than I could count. Sometimes it seemed as if he enjoyed provoking and sparring. He'd assure me that one day I would work for him.

So far, that hadn't happened.

But today, there was something I couldn't put my finger on. A different air about him. He was a confident man. Always.

I usually left any encounter with him beyond angry. Blindingly mad.

Now . . . I was unsettled.

Was I just a puppet in his game? Had I been all along?

I didn't know the rules. Had he given me the illusion of free will, allowing me to believe I had the power over my own life?

That seemed crazy. Ultimately, the only way he could control me was by threatening the people and things I cared about.

Which was how he won today.

He'd held my career over my head all these years, but there was an end game, even if I didn't know what it was.

What he'd done to Pepper, Miss Adeline, and the dogs was unacceptable. But I firmly believed he'd make good on his promises to shut them down. What I wasn't sure of was if that held beyond getting me to his office earlier.

Could I go back?

As I climbed into my truck, all I wanted was to see her. Apologize . . . for everything.

I couldn't risk it. I wouldn't be responsible for the destruction of her world.

Because my father would do it just to make me suffer.

How he knew about her, how he seemed to know more about my feelings for her than I did, was incomprehensible.

I rested my forehead on the steering wheel.

I needed to crash at my brother's place. If I went home, I'd be too tempted to see Pepper.

What she didn't know was the day we met, I'd moved into the building next door.

CHAPTER TWENTY-ONE

PEPPER

"UMM, CAN I HELP YOU?"

I set my pencil down on the legal pad. Two men in dark clothes set down the large box they carried.

"Where would you like the kennels set up?" one of them asked in a thick Brooklyn accent.

"I beg your pardon?"

"The kennels? We're here to set them up."

The front door opened and two more men carried another box.

"Yo, Rivera. Move it so we can get in."

"I'm trying to find out where the lady wants them so I don't have to pick up this giant ass box more times than I have to," Brooklyn fired back.

"You need to lift it a lot so I can stop pulling your weight."

"I'm the one carrying you."

"Bullshit. The only thing you beat me at is eating all the leftovers."

"You calling me fat?"

A shrill whistle pierced the air.

Sadie, who'd been peacefully sleeping at my feet, sat up. Thank goodness the other dogs were in the back with Miss Adeline.

"You're letting all the warm air out," one of the other men who hadn't been arguing said. "Move."

Brooklyn grumbled as he picked up his end of the box.

"Wait." I stood. "I think you're at the wrong address. I haven't ordered any kennels."

"This is Grey Paws, right?"

I nodded. "Yes."

"Then we're in the right place." Brooklyn set down the box again once the others had room to get inside.

"I—I don't understand."

"We're here to set these up." The man looked around as if trying to figure out where they would go.

As he turned, I saw the FDNY logo on the back of his T-shirt.

"Who sent you?" I asked carefully.

They all looked at one another. Suddenly, they were silent.

There were two possibilities. Teague. Or Miss Adeline. While Miss Adeline calling firemen was a good option, my money was on Teague.

It hurt to think about him. About yesterday.

His horrible father.

The way he'd been forced to obey. And that in itself, when I considered Lincoln and Beau—their obvious strength and confidence —I was amazed. I'd thought Lincoln had been cool, unaffected, aloof, but he had nothing on his father. And Beau, gloriously coolheaded and unflappable, had acquiesced just as quickly as Lincoln. Who was that man? And how were they his children?

After a night to process what had happened, it was clear he'd only done as his father demanded because of me. And the dogs.

I was rattled.

Teague had nothing in common with that man beyond looks. I couldn't imagine him ever threatening to destroy a complete stranger's livelihood.

But there was no doubt in my mind that his father would do that and more without a second thought.

"Ma'am, we'd love to get started." The man who hadn't yet spoken finally did with a gentle voice.

I scratched my head. We'd never set up kennels in the front because of the windows. And we wanted to have a reception area.

But the back was full. There was no choice but here.

I pointed along the wall to my left. "Start there please."

They immediately bolted into action, opening the boxes and removing the pieces from inside them.

"Would it be okay if we move the desk over there?" Brooklyn asked. "That'll make more room along this long wall."

"Sure. Anything you need." I poked my head in the back room. "Some friends of yours are here."

Miss Adeline furrowed her brow but wasted no time coming to see what I was talking about.

"Hello, boys. So nice of you to join us." Had she arranged this? She certainly didn't seem surprised to see them. "Would you like something cold to drink?"

"No thank you," they choroused.

"Did you know they were coming?" I whispered.

"Nope. But I'm sure not going to turn them away." Her eyes were glued to one bent over.

I elbowed her in the side. "Stop ogling."

"You don't mind an old lady enjoying the view, right?"

Their faces turned scarlet, and I cringed.

"Stop calling yourself an old lady."

"I *am* an old lady."

"I'm always up for a beautiful woman appreciating my assets," Brooklyn said with a cheeky grin.

"I just adore Mr. February."

He winked.

She had the calendar men memorized.

"My real name is Anthony Rivera. That's Logan Burke. Mason Walsh. And Sean Scavino."

"We are so glad you're here and stay as long as you like," she said.

"Were you always this flirty?" I asked.

Sadie cocked her head as if she wanted to hear the answer too.

"I'm charming. Not flirty." She placed a hand on her hip . . . and kept staring.

Now I could see they all had some sort of FDNY shirt on. "Are you sure you didn't know they were coming?"

There was more accusation in my tone than question.

She held up both her hands. "No clue. I swear."

The woman was the picture of innocence. But I knew when she fibbed. The corner of her mouth moved when she did. It was still.

"I have a pretty good idea who did though." She tickled my side and I yelped.

All the firemen glanced in our direction but continued working.

She put an arm around my waist. "He'll be back."

I wasn't entirely sure of that, and the thought unsettled me. In a few short days, I'd grown used to him popping up just when I needed him most. I should've been stronger than that.

"It doesn't matter," I said. Did it? Was I lying to myself?

"If you say so."

"PIZZA'S HERE."

The bell jangled when Miss Adeline barged through carrying three large boxes from Dino's.

I moved the tools and papers sitting on the desk to clear out a space. The guys dropped what they were doing, and I showed them to the sink where they could wash their hands.

They waded through the dogs, who were all out of their kennels, and were good-natured about the jumps, barks, and licks they endured. Brooklyn even threw a couple of balls on his way, which were hastily retrieved.

"You've started something you might not have meant to," I said when Millie happily trotted back to him, ball in mouth.

A tug of war ensued. Brooklyn eventually wrestled the ball away from her and tossed it again.

"They're really great," he said as he washed his hands.

I appreciated those words so very much. "They are."

"I'll throw it again after I eat," he said when Millie returned with the ball.

Miss Adeline had the spread arranged on the desk. No one bothered with a plate. We all dove in and I found myself wishing Teague and Beau were with us.

I enjoyed having them around yesterday. The dogs liked it too. They liked having the firemen here. Maybe we should try to get more volunteers to give them one-on-one time.

"Tell us about Teague."

I nearly choked on my pizza at Miss Adeline's question.

"Does he date much?"

"I thought you liked me?" Brooklyn sounded affronted.

She tilted her head toward me. He nodded in an *I gotcha* kind of way.

It appeared to be her life's mission to embarrass the heck out of me.

"I don't remember him seeing anyone since I've known him. We went through training together." Logan ripped off a bite of pizza.

"Me neither. We've been at the same station for nine years," Mason added.

"He's kinda private though. He's close with his brother and sister, but he's one of those people who can keep the focus on you, if that makes sense."

Sean pointed and finished chewing. "Yeah. We work with him every day. He's our brother. We know him, but it's like surface stuff."

"He's the best cook at the house. That's all I need to know," Brooklyn said.

Logan patted his round stomach. "We see that."

They all laughed. Brooklyn wadded up a napkin and threw it at him.

"Just wait until you're pushing fifty."

"I've got a long way to go before that," Logan shot back, then he turned serious. "Teague's always the first one to volunteer for anything. He never complains. I trust him with my life. I can't say that about everyone."

They all hummed their agreement.

"I'm ready for that bastard to get back. It's bullshit they suspended him."

Suspended? I thought he was taking time off.

"You didn't know," Logan said.

My face must've given away my shock. I shook my head.

"He didn't do anything wrong. Captain has it out for him. Always riding his ass." Mason snorted in disgust.

Sadie nudged his hand with the pizza in it.

"Sadie. No," I said. She bumped him again.

"Sorry, sweetheart," he said.

She was undeterred. She sat on his foot and stared up at him.

It was impossible to get mad when she was so funny.

"Did Teague send you to do this?" I asked, a little afraid of the answer and how it would make me feel.

They looked around at each other just as they had before.

"We've been sworn to secrecy," Brooklyn said. "But we're not to leave until you're all set up and happy."

He'd done it.

He cared enough about these dogs to make sure they were comfortable and safe. The kennels weren't cages. They were a space for them to make their own.

Everyone liked to have their own room.

That was what he'd given them.

And I wasn't sure when I'd ever see him again to thank him.

I went to the back and mixed up the clay we used to make paw imprints for people who donated and adopted our dogs.

I coaxed Ash over and pressed her paw into the soft material. She complied without hesitation. I placed it in a box and set it beside Brooklyn.

"Will you make sure he gets this?"

Even if I never had anything to do with him, I wanted him to have a part of Grey Paws. And Ash. And maybe, he'd know that he was getting a part of me too. Something I rarely gave away.

CHAPTER TWENTY-TWO

TEAGUE

"IS something wrong with your new place?"

Lincoln leaned on the door frame of the guest room I'd claimed.

"Yeah. But I don't want to get into it." I pulled a shirt over my head. "Want to grab a beer?"

"Mind if we do it here? I . . . I've had enough of out there for one day." He motioned toward the windows.

Right on cue, a car horn blared, followed by a second one. I was ready to escape the noise of the outside world too.

"Fine by me."

I followed him to the living room. He plunked a few ice cubes in two tumblers and poured amber liquid over the top.

"Hope something stronger is okay." He handed me a glass.

"Better than okay."

We sat in silence for a minute, sipping our whiskey. Lincoln sank lower in the chair and spread his legs. I rarely saw him completely relax. He was on guard and put together at all times.

He loosened his tie and dropped his head to the back of the chair.

"What's his deal?"

There was no need to elaborate on who I meant.

He sighed. "I don't know."

"I don't want you and Beau to shield me anymore." I'd thought of barely anything else all day. It wasn't fair that I pursued what I wanted while they were stuck as our father's puppets. The problem was, I didn't know how to fix it.

He snapped his gaze toward me. "Are you coming to work for Hollingsworth Properties?"

I recoiled. "No. I—" I ran a hand through my hair. "I don't know what I'm doing."

"He's not going to let this go."

He'd allowed me to walk out of his office relatively easy, but my brother was right.

"If I . . ." I hesitated over the words I needed to get out. They were harder to speak than I thought. "Take him up, will that make things easier on you?"

My brother closed his eyes. "That's not how it works and you know it."

"How does it work?"

"He barks. You dance. He bitches." Beau joined us and tossed her purse on the floor then grabbed Lincoln's glass. She downed it in one swallow and wiped her mouth with the back of her hand.

She kicked off her shoes and brought the bottle of whiskey over. After she topped off both of our glasses, she collapsed on the sofa next to me.

"You forgot he kicks you in the nuts." Blindly, he brought his glass up to his lips.

"How could I forget that?" Beau snatched my tumbler out of my hand. "Don't even think about it, Teague. He makes it sound like doing what he wants is easiest, but it's not."

"Disobeying is pretty damn hard too." I slouched and grabbed my glass back.

"I've been here two days and I already remember why I live in London."

"Do you honestly think an ocean deters him?" Lincoln asked.

"A little. Some barrier is better than none at all." She propped her feet on the coffee table. "What are you going to do about Pepper?"

I'd tried to shove her out of my mind, but it was hard.

"What can I do? You heard him." There was pure hatred in my voice. I didn't like that, didn't want to feel that way.

"I like her."

That made two of us. Maybe I should be grateful that my father had inserted himself before I got to know her better. It would've hurt worse later. What I still didn't know was how he found out about Grey Paws, and how he knew Pepper meant something to me.

The man had an uncanny gift for sensing when I was happy and doing anything to destroy that.

"If you so much as speak her name, he'll shut that place down." Lincoln stared at the ceiling, his tone flat.

"I know."

"I'm sorry."

I jerked my gaze toward him. He wasn't unfeeling, but it was so rare to hear those words out of his mouth.

I slumped further and mirrored his position.

"Me too."

"So what? You just give her up?" In the complete opposite fashion of our brother, Beau's tone was full of passion.

"I don't know." I focused on the glass I held. "I just met her. Why drag her into unnecessary hell?"

"You can't let him shut them down," Beau said resolutely.

"Of course I won't," I snapped. The only way I knew to do that was to stay away from her. Even that wasn't a sure-fire method.

"Just because you can't see her, doesn't mean you can't be there." She reached for the glass.

"How?"

"Like what you did today. Sending the guys to set up the kennels." She bumped my shoulder like she was proud of me.

"I should've been there."

Fresh bitterness washed over me. I'd wanted to assemble those kennels. He'd taken that away from me.

"You can't go near her." Lincoln set his glass on the coffee table.

"How am I going to avoid it when I live next door?"

"What?" Beau sat up straight and twisted to face me. I nodded. "That's perfect. You can't help if you 'run into her' if she's your neighbor."

Her excitement was contagious . . . and dangerous. I didn't trust myself in close proximity to Grey Paws. It was too tempting.

"Don't do that to her." My brother was like a cold bucket of water dumped over my head.

He was right.

"Mind if I stay here while I figure some things out?" I was a coward. Samuel Hollingsworth controlled me even when he wasn't around.

Every move in my life was done with him in mind.

"You never have to ask."

I flicked my chin at him in gratitude. What would I do without these two?

"I get to keep my own bathroom." Beau did a little happy dance. I smacked my knee against hers. She threw a piece of ice at me, which I caught and popped into my mouth. As I crunched, she gripped my thigh, her expression turning serious. "What he said today . . . he was out of line. She wanted all of us to be happy."

A searing pain knifed through my chest. Beau had been too young to really know how our mother would've felt. Hell, I didn't know either and I'd been her shadow.

She was gone. And there was nothing that would change that.

I glanced around at all of our sullen faces.

"Then why are we all so miserable?"

CHAPTER TWENTY-THREE

PEPPER

THIS IS STUPID.

I hesitated and ducked behind a building out of the wind. Five days had passed since the guys had put together the kennels. The dogs were happy with their new safe spaces . . . and the daily barrage of treats and toys that had followed.

I hadn't seen or heard from Teague. Not that I'd expected to.

But he was present in every squeak of a toy, every crunch of one of Garrison's dog biscuits, and every lap of water out of one of the new bowls that had magically appeared.

I peered around the corner. The firehouse door was up. A couple of guys I didn't recognize milled around out front. I should've brought Miss Adeline. She'd recognize them from the calendar.

Why I'd woken bound and determined to thank Teague in person was beyond me. I was grateful for all he'd done. It felt wrong to be showered with his gifts and not find a way to express my gratitude.

All it took was a little reconnaissance work from Miss Adeline's new fans to find him. He was back at work. And this was the station.

Nerves spiked as I stared at the firehouse.

I looked down at my overalls.

Why hadn't I changed clothes before I set off on this crazy endeavor?

Because as soon as Miss Adeline found out what I was up to, she'd shoved me out the door. The woman knew me too well. I'd overthink and lose my courage.

Like I was now.

"Just go over there." Now I'd resorted to talking to myself. Great.

Yet my feet didn't move.

What if he didn't want to see me?

He's been sending deliveries every day. For the dogs. Not me.

But I was an extension of them. And if they couldn't say their thanks, I would.

I took a step forward. Then another.

How did he afford all this stuff? Nothing he'd sent was cheap. I'd overheard the guys mention they hadn't had a pay raise in three years.

Obviously his family looked as if they had money, but that didn't mean Teague did.

"Yo. Pepper."

Too late to back out now.

"Hey, Logan." I waved awkwardly.

He pulled me in for a giant bear hug. "Scavino. Walsh. Look who's here."

I was passed between them like a ping-pong ball in the tournament of hugs. When it was over, I stood there with flamed cheeks, insecure despite the warm welcome.

"How do the dogs like the kennels?" Walsh asked.

"They love them. Thank you," I said quietly.

"Them things haven't fallen down, right?" Brooklyn barreled into the group and I got another hug.

"Still standing." I crossed my fingers and they all laughed.

"She ain't here to see us." Logan nudged my arm.

I blushed.

"Pepper?" Teague stood by the front of the fire engine. His expression was one of disbelief and I wasn't sure what else.

It wasn't the warm welcome I'd hoped for.

Logan gently pushed me toward him.

"Hi." I shook my head. "I should've called or something before I came by."

Teague ushered me into a corner as if he were hiding me. Or didn't want to be seen with me.

"Woo Hoo!" The guys cheered.

Maybe Miss Adeline had passed on the mission to embarrass me to them.

"What are you doing here?" he asked sharply.

I stiffened. "I—I wanted to thank you."

He folded his arms, his muscles bulging when he did. I shivered. How did he have on a T-shirt in this cold?

"There's nothing to thank me for," he said to the ground.

"I know it was you who arranged for the kennels. And the entertaining crew." I motioned toward the guys, who were still gathered together. "All kinds of things arrive every day. They never did before we met you, so there's only one option."

He remained silent and refused to meet my gaze.

"The three dogs from the track in Jersey . . . they're home from the vet. They're going to be okay." I'd picked them up yesterday. The road was going to be long, especially for Lucky. His leg was badly fractured, but Dr. Lyons promised he'd make a full recovery.

"That's great news," he said flatly.

"I—" I waffled between speaking my mind and tucking tail. Usually, I remained quiet. At some point, I had to learn to be brave. "I'm sorry your father put you in that position."

He looked at me incredulously. "You're sorry? He threatened you. He kicked Muffy." He plowed a hand through his hair. "There aren't enough apologies in the world to make up for what he did. And none of them should be coming from you."

"How he treats you—"

"What about how he treated you?" he roared.

I recoiled, startled by his anger. "We'll be fine."

"You shouldn't be here. You have no idea who he is or what he's capable of." He stalked past me.

"Thank you."

He paused but kept his back to me. His shoulders heaved as if he was taking ragged breaths.

This hadn't gone how I'd hoped. I wasn't sure what I'd wanted exactly, but I'd come here to express my gratitude. At least I'd accomplished that.

Slowly he turned, but he came no closer. His eyes that had been unreadable before were now filled with pain. I'd seen so many expressions on this man's face. Some hadn't made sense, and when I thought he'd been a jerk, I realized that he'd simply been angry. And now that I thought about it, I was sure he mentioned that he'd been on an unpleasant call. With his dad? But over time, I'd seen so many more expressions, and I'd begun to like every one of them. Even when he'd been fired up about his dad's presence—that had been attractive. But this one? This was sorrow mixed with anger. Pain mixed with sad resolution. Disappointment.

"Don't lose everything you love over me. I'm not worth it."

CHAPTER TWENTY-FOUR

TEAGUE

"YOU'RE AN ASSHOLE."

Burke punched me in the arm as Pepper hurried away with her head down. She'd barely acknowledged any of them as she'd passed.

"What's new?" I pretended to check that everything was good to go on the truck. It was a poor means of distraction, but I was desperate to do anything but watch her walk away.

"That's not you, man."

I slammed one of the cubby doors. "Maybe it is and I'm just good at hiding it."

Anger pumped through my veins. I was mad at Pepper for risking being seen with me. I was mad at my father for his tentacles that seemed to have no bounds. I was mad at Burke for calling me out.

Most of all, I was angry with myself. For being a jerk to her. For not standing up for myself. For being deluded enough to believe my life had been my own.

A massive hand clamped on my shoulder. "I don't know why you just treated her that way, but I'm going to give you the benefit of the doubt that there was a good reason."

And then I was surrounded by my friends. Should've known if I sent them to help out at Grey Paws they'd end up as smitten as I was.

"You owe her an apology." Rivera scolded me in his thick Brooklyn accent. "Like now."

They shoved me in her direction.

I couldn't argue with them when they were right, but they didn't know why it was risky. My father obviously had eyes on me . . . a lot.

Another shove. And another. Until they'd pushed me out the garage door.

Screw it.

I jogged in the direction she'd taken off in.

Riiiiiiiiiinnnnnnggggggg.

Damn it. The alarm jolted me back toward the station.

I'd been off seven days. It took a second for my muscle memory to kick in, but once it did, I moved on autopilot.

This was what I knew. What I was comfortable with. The process.

Suit up.

Grab helmet.

Get in truck.

Put on earphones.

"One alarm. Sixth Street. Persons inside unknown."

That wasn't far from Grey Paws. A few blocks. Panic I wasn't used to wound its way into my chest.

I had my routine. I was levelheaded when it came to emergency calls.

They'd be fine. But it was too close for comfort.

The sirens wailed as we raced through the streets. I'd always liked that sound. It meant help was on the way. I'd become a fireman because I wanted to help people.

Would my father have been happier if I'd become a doctor?

No. I wouldn't think of him now. Wouldn't let him infiltrate the career I took great pride in.

The blaze came into view. A dumpster was engulfed. Flames licked up the side of the brick building beside it.

Bystanders had gathered with buckets and hoses and curious eyes.

I had the door open before we rolled to a stop and immediately unleashed the hose. Burke helped me drag it toward the hydrant as Walsh removed the cap so we could hook up.

"Thank you for the help, but stand back everyone." I ushered the people to the opposite side of the street.

Embers floated up into the sky as the fire raged.

A blast of water pelted the dumpster.

Boom.

An explosion lifted it off the ground. It landed with a clang as glass and metal and trash rained down.

Screams filled the air. People scurried and panicked.

I ducked and covered my head. The guys on the hose never stopped spraying.

Thwack.

Something landed in front of me. I leaned forward to examine whatever it was. It was charred, almost like a small log.

I nudged it with my boot.

Was that . . . a foot?

I stepped back. "Burke. Get over here."

He jogged over. "Yo."

I pointed at the object, pretty sure that was a toenail hanging off.

"What the hell?" He squatted down. "That's a freaking foot."

At least I wasn't imagining things. Although, I wished I was.

Another piece of debris caught my gaze a few yards away. I hustled over. "Here's a hand."

"Oh damn. You think somebody was in that dumpster?" Burke said over the comms.

"Burke. Keep this channel clear," Captain Koker snapped.

Damn. When did he get here? I'd hoped to avoid him . . . forever.

He strolled toward us and crooked his finger. "Don't say shit like that over the comms."

It would all be public record soon enough anyway. Why not let some nosy reporter who was listening help authorities get the jump on solving what appeared to be a crime?

"Looks like we need to call in homicide," I said.

"This could be some homeless person in the wrong place at the wrong time." He made a disgruntled noise. "Crime unit is en route. I want a report on my desk tonight."

He stalked off.

Burke rolled his eyes. "Me and my big mouth."

"It won't take long to write." I scanned the area. "'Contained bystanders. Dumpster exploded. Foot landed in front of me.' That should about cover it."

"You left out 'Got ass chewed by Captain.'"

I grinned. "Yeah. Don't let me forget that part."

"Are you two gonna help put out this blaze or stand around all afternoon?" Rivera called.

"Looks like you've got it covered," Burke said before he fist-bumped me. "We're just over here dodging body parts."

Some guys didn't mind the gruesome stuff. I dealt with it, but knowing there were pieces of someone scattered around bothered me. Had they been alive when the fire started? Had they been dumped first? Had they started the fire to keep warm and it got out of control?

Once the investigators took over, the questions were likely ones I'd never know the answers to. Sure, we gossiped around the station, but so often we were on to the next one.

I'd gotten good at sweeping the things I'd seen from my mind over the years. When I first started, I carried every single call with me. If I'd stayed on that path, I'd have never made it this long.

But sometimes those things that were long forgotten would creep up unexpectedly.

I scanned the scene against my better judgment, cataloguing every detail. The sequence of autopilot events had been broken with the explosion. Deviating was what would get me in trouble later. Because I'd remember.

And then my mind would wander with a million questions.

"Yo." Burke said that word so much I was surprised I didn't say it on repeat. "Blaze is out. Help me roll up the hoses."

I appreciated him saving me from my own self-destruction. In this line of work, there had to be a wall of separation between the job and personal life. Unfortunately, my wall was made of glass instead of concrete.

Do not think about this later.

As I tried to sweep everything I'd just seen from my head, I noticed a dark car easing away from the curb down the street.

And it looked an awful lot like my father's.

CHAPTER TWENTY-FIVE

PEPPER

"SWEETHEART, YOU HAVE TO EAT."

I sat in Ash's kennel with a bowl of food in front of me. She refused to lift her head, no matter how I coaxed.

For two days, she hadn't eaten. I'd gotten a little water into her by dipping my finger into the bowl and putting it on her tongue. She'd go outside and didn't appear to be injured.

But I was about to the point of calling Dr. Lyons.

"What's the matter? Do you feel bad?"

She blew out a heavy breath through her nostrils. I stroked her head and she closed her eyes.

Sadie stuck her nose through the fenced wall that separated them and sniffed.

"You can't have her dinner," I said.

She sat down, more determined now that I'd scolded her. She pawed at the fence.

"No, Sadie."

She kept right on and I wondered if she wanted to get to Ash.

"I can't believe I'm falling for this," I muttered as I stood.

I opened Sadie's kennel and she trotted right into Ash's. Past the food. And she lay down beside her.

"Sure. Make me look bad for thinking the worst." I sat again. "But you brought it on yourself."

Her nose worked overtime, inching closer and closer to the bowl. She licked her lips and snuck a swipe at the food.

I moved it away before she reached it. "You already had yours."

She rested her head on Ash's neck and it was so sweet I instantly forgave her.

I put a little of the gourmet food—there really was no other way to describe what Beau's friend Lexie brought over every day—on my fingers. Ash sniffed when I held it up to her mouth but refused to eat it.

Wet tongue hit my fingers . . . but it was the wrong one. Sadie smacked on the food and put her head back down.

"You are something else."

I tried to get Ash to drink. All I got was another heavy sigh.

I reached into my memories of the past several days and tried to remember when this started. The last time I recalled her eating was a couple days after the guys came to set up the new kennels.

When she was out of her kennel, she always went straight to the door and stared out the glass. Like she was looking for something.

Or someone.

"Teague."

Her ears perked up at his name. She glanced toward the front room hopefully. When he wasn't there, she rolled over on her side.

Poor girl. She'd lost her owners and now she'd lost her friend.

"Miss Adeline," I called.

She rolled her chair into the doorway. "She still won't eat?"

"Get your black book out and your charm ready."

She tilted her head. "Are you feeling okay?"

"If you pull this off, I'll feel amazing."

———

ASH TRUDGED beside me as we walked to the park. I darted my gaze from one side of the street to another and tried to see in every parked car.

This was a risk. But one I had to take for my girl.

I imagined this was what a drug deal felt like. Except I had a bowl and a baggie of food in my bag.

When the entrance to the park came into view, my heart rate accelerated. It was beyond cold out. No one was crazy enough to be hanging out there, even to walk their dog.

We should've come up with a better place. More secluded than this.

Paranoia took over as we crossed the street into the park. I guided us to a bench, paced back and forth a few times before I finally sat.

Ash looked at me with a *what are we doing here* expression.

"I'm not sure," I said.

We were early, but I'd been too anxious to wait any longer. Now that I'd exposed us to the elements, I regretted that decision.

The cold cut through my gloves. Ash didn't seem to notice that it was freezing.

We sat for what felt like an eternity. I checked my phone and it had only been ten minutes since we'd left home.

Ash stared at me. She grew tired of standing and sat at my feet.

I hadn't told her what we were doing because I didn't want to get her hopes up. Contrary to what most people thought, dogs could speak some English.

I checked the time again.

Five minutes had passed.

I looked around as my anxiety increased. If he didn't show, I didn't know what I was going to do.

Every second felt like a lifetime. I tapped the screen on my phone again. Only another minute had gone by.

Ash stamped her paws.

"I know it's cold. But let's just wait a little more."

He was late.

Maybe Miss Adeline wasn't as convincing as I thought.

I tried to control the interval with which I tapped the phone screen but failed. Instead I'd increased to twice a minute. Another seven had gone by. Still no sign.

He's not coming.

I didn't want to voice that out loud. Didn't want to disappoint Ash.

"Just another few minutes," I said quietly through chattering teeth.

She shivered. We couldn't stay much longer. I wouldn't risk her already fragile health.

I cupped her face and kissed the top of her head. She nuzzled against me.

"I'm sorry, sweet girl. I thought—"

She leapt up and yanked on the leash, her tail wagging.

In the distance, a familiar form approached.

Tall. Muscular. Long, quick strides.

The closer he got, the harder she pulled. I couldn't believe she had the strength. She nearly jerked me off the bench.

When he was on park grounds, I freed her.

She rocketed toward Teague and jumped when she reached him. He caught her paws and placed them on his stomach so he could rub down her sides.

She squealed and squeaked. He squatted, and she peppered his face with kisses.

I took in the scene with a full heart, the cold forgotten. The moment was bittersweet. We couldn't stay out here forever. What would we do tomorrow and the next day and the day after that when she couldn't see him?

I'd have to worry about that later.

He rose to his full height. She jumped again but followed happily as he strode toward me. With every step, my heart drummed in my chest in a pounding rhythm.

The last time I'd seen him hadn't gone well. I was more hurt than angry over it, but in a lot of ways I was as thrilled to see him as Ash.

The brim of his baseball cap was low over his eyes so I couldn't read his expression. When he reached the bench, I stopped breathing.

We stared at one another. A crackling snapped between us. He continued petting Ash, but his sharp gaze was locked on me.

"Pepper." My name was a hoarse plea on his lips.

"Teague," I replied softly.

Ash licked my knee in thanks, which jolted me back to reality. I scooted over to make room for him on the bench but put my bag so it would be between us.

I was afraid to be any closer to him than I had to be. Because like Ash, I'd missed him too.

He sat wordlessly. I pulled out the bowl, baggie of food, and a bottle of water.

"Thank you," I said as I emptied the food into the bowl.

He held it in his lap. Ash gobbled it down in three point five seconds. Relief coursed through me at the same time worry did. Maybe we'd figured out why she wasn't eating, and I might be able to get something in her in the morning, but what happened after that? Teague wouldn't be able to do this every day.

I couldn't ask him to foster her. She needed a forever home, not a temporary place she became attached to and then lost. That wouldn't be fair to her. We'd just have to work through her separation issues until she was happy.

"I'm sorry." He turned his head to me. The apology was in every line of his face.

"It's—" I didn't want to say okay because that was a lie. He'd been rude to me at the fire station, just like he had the first day we met. Even though I knew the root of the issue, I didn't appreciate it.

"I don't get scared," he said before I decided how to finish my sentence. "But when he threatened you? I was terrified."

My heart cracked at his concern.

"I can't be the one to screw up your life."

I put a hand on his knee, my bag barrier be damned. He stiffened and looked around in every direction as if paranoid. That set me on edge, but I took comfort that he didn't dismiss my touch.

"I hated to put you in this position, but I was desperate. She wouldn't eat." I pressed my lips together when Ash pawed at his hand. "Now we know why."

He leaned forward and touched his nose to her head. "I missed you too."

Whatever anger and hurt I held onto shattered. This was the real Teague. I didn't know how many people got to see this stripped down, authentic version of him. Heck, *I* didn't even know him all that well. But I was certain. The sensitive man who met me in a freezing park on the chance he could get a dog to eat was the true version of himself.

She swiped at his chin and anywhere she could reach with her tongue. He didn't seem to mind she had dog food breath.

He sat back straight but kept petting her.

"Mind seeing if you can get some water in her?" I poured a little into the bowl.

He didn't even have to coax her. She lapped gently until it was gone. I poured a little more and she mopped it up too.

The pressure that had been on my chest since she'd stopped eating eased. She'd eaten. And she was happy.

We sat in silence for a long time. Ash was content to be nestled between Teague's legs. I was fine with prolonging the moment too.

"I should go," he finally said, though he made no move.

Everything in me rebelled at that. I wanted to ask him to come home with me, have supper, maybe take the dogs for their evening walk. Instead I stayed statue still.

Regret washed over his features. His strokes became stilted. Ash looked up at him as if she knew time was short. She put her head on his leg in a *you're not going anywhere* gesture.

"I can't do this every day."

"I wouldn't ask that of you." And I wouldn't. He had a life. He wasn't responsible for me or the dogs.

We always found our way and we would again.

He brushed his thumb across my cheek. I closed my eyes.

"In another life . . ." he said hoarsely.

"This is the one we have." I gathered the bowl and put it back in the plastic sack before shoving it into my bag. "Ready to go home, Ash?"

I stood. She remained sitting on Teague's foot. The next step would be her wrapping her paws around his leg and refusing to leave.

I hoped it didn't come to that.

Reluctantly, he rose. As predicted, Ash still didn't move, literally glued to him.

He looked at me helplessly. I lifted a shoulder and lowered it. There was no good answer.

"Will you let her sleep with you tonight?"

I was caught off guard by the request but nodded. Gently, I tugged on the leash. She wouldn't budge.

Teague unwrapped the scarf around his neck and held it out to me. "It's only fair since I have her paw print."

Oh God. My chest tightened painfully when he patted his pocket. Did he have the imprint with him? Had he the other day?

I swallowed hard, my throat too clogged to speak as I accepted the scarf.

He bent to kiss Ash's head and whispered something against her fur.

A crushing sensation walloped my heart. She whimpered, as if she knew this was goodbye.

He flicked his chin at me and walked off without looking back. Ash struggled to chase after him, even pulling me a few feet. She barked until he was out of sight. No words I used to try to calm her worked.

I wrapped the scarf around her neck, hoping Teague's scent would soothe her.

Ash tried to pull me in the direction he'd gone but eventually conceded to heading home.

I knew without a doubt she wouldn't eat until she saw him again.

CHAPTER TWENTY-SIX

TEAGUE

I EMPTIED my pockets onto the dresser.

When my fingers grazed the mold of Ash's paw, pain and anger stabbed at my chest. Trauma had a way of bringing people—and animals—together. We'd gone through the same fire. That gave us a connection very few could understand.

But I'd never expected she wouldn't eat because of me.

When had anyone ever cared enough to stop eating because I wasn't around?

The only person who might've come close was my mother. I hadn't been able to keep anything down after she'd died. Grief and horror had nearly overtaken me . . . and I'd only been five.

Beau and Lincoln hadn't taken it well either. Maybe that was why the three of us were so close. The shared loss.

I had no doubt they'd be upset if something ever happened to me, but seeing Ash strain to get to me and the way she'd jumped all over me once she did . . . I'd never known a feeling like that.

It was one I still couldn't quite wrap my mind around.

That sense of being needed . . . I realized I'd been missing that.

Which was crazy. I had the guys at the firehouse. I had my family. It wasn't like I was lonely and isolated.

Nevertheless, I'd never forget that bittersweet moment.

And Pepper.

Her reception had been more reserved. Truthfully, I'd been stunned to see her. Miss Adeline had called the station, and I hadn't been able to say no when she told me Ash wasn't eating, consequences be damned.

There'd been so many things I'd wanted to say to Pepper. But I hadn't been able to think of a damn one of them. Even underneath the veil of worry, she'd been as beautiful as ever.

I was sure contacting me had been a last resort. Yet I admired how in tune she was with the dogs. How she'd put together Ash wasn't eating because of me was incredible. Only someone who loved those animals would be able to do that.

The entire scene hadn't lasted long, but I'd been drained when I left. Emotionally. Mentally. Physically.

Seeing those two had been a jolt of energy and the ultimate crash when I'd left them. I wanted to call Pepper to see how Ash was doing —how *she* was doing. But I wouldn't push my luck.

Knock. Knock.

My sister stood in the partially opened doorway to my room, looking as drained as I felt.

"What happened to you?" She made herself at home and sat on the bed.

"I could ask you the same." I reached behind me and pulled off my sweater and undershirt.

I rifled through my bag until I found a fresh T-shirt.

"Please don't change your pants in front of me," she groaned.

"You're the one who barged in my room."

"Remind me not to do that again." She collapsed sideways onto the mattress.

"Lincoln home?"

"I don't think so. But I haven't seen him all day. Dad's had me shadowing him like I'm his personal assistant." Her head lolled to the side.

I sat in the corner chair. "You never did take orders well."

"Like you did either," she shot back and then sighed. "I've been with that man for twelve hours and the only thing I learned is I put too much sugar in his coffee."

I could barely spend twelve minutes with him. How she'd with-stood that long was a testament to her strength.

"What were you expecting to find out?" I yanked off my boots and tossed them to the side.

"Why he's pressuring you to work at the company."

I sat straighter. "Did you ask him?"

Her gaze was cutting. "No. I'm not an idiot."

"I didn't say you were." My patience was quickly wearing thin.

I'd seen an exploded body. Gotten a reaming from the captain in front of everyone. And then there was the whole thing with Pepper. I didn't have the mental energy to fish for information from Beau.

"It's been a while, hasn't it? Since he pushed."

I thought back. "Maybe a year."

Time ran together and he'd demanded so much I'd lost count.

She put a hand to her forehead. "There's something going on. First, he drags me back here—"

"You mean the trip wasn't something you wanted?"

Guilt morphed her features. "No."

I figured her being back in New York was business-related first, but knowing she had no desire to be here, to see Lincoln and me? It felt like she'd slapped me.

"I see how it is." I couldn't look at her.

"Teague. It's not you and Lincoln. I love you both more than anything."

"Then why'd you run away?"

I understood needing distance and separation from our father, but she'd moved half a world away.

"I didn't run away. I ran *to* London."

My gaze snapped to her. What could've possibly drawn her there of all places? She'd done a study abroad program in college over in Europe, but she'd never mentioned any ties.

I'd always prided myself on how close I was to my siblings. We knew practically everything about each other. At least I thought we did.

"Don't get that wounded puppy look." She sat up.

"I'm just trying to figure out what I'm missing."

The ink had barely dried on her master's diploma before she'd convinced our father to set up operations in London and hopped a flight to spearhead the entire endeavor.

"Don't bother." She slapped her palms on the edge of the bed and pushed up. "I'm calling it a night."

I caught her hand as she passed. "I know I'm your brother and there are things you'd probably rather keep from me." She smirked, and I squeezed her fingers. "But you can talk to me. About anything."

She squeezed back. "Same goes."

"I Got You Babe" blared from the direction of the dresser.

Beau snorted. "Do you choose these ringtones?" She swiped my phone and dropped it into my lap.

Burke's name flashed on the screen.

"You bastard. How'd you figure out my passcode again?" I laughed, more amused than annoyed.

A rustling came from the other end of the phone instead of a return jab. He cleared his throat.

"Cassano is dead."

CHAPTER TWENTY-SEVEN

TEAGUE

THE PHONE FELL from my grasp onto the carpet.

"Yo. Teague."

I dropped my chin to my chest.

Beau picked up the device and held it to her ear. She murmured and nodded, though her face was ashen.

Cassano is dead.

Cassano. Is. Dead.

I'd seen him a few days ago. We'd joked about who cooked a better chili. He'd been determined to get back to work in a few weeks.

"DOC SAYS *I'm doing better than expected." He grinned. "I'll be back making your sorry ass look bad again in no time."*

"You better. Captain's getting bored with only having me to peg stuff on."

He flipped me the bird.

"He's really going to be after you when he hears your next ringtone. I'll be calling you nonstop."

. . .

HE HAD. TWO DAYS AGO. "BELIEVE" had repeated so much Captain turned off my phone. And someone had already changed the ringtone.

How could a person playing pranks just the other day be gone now?

Beau ended the call and sat on the arm of the chair. "Heart attack. They're not sure what caused it yet."

"He was thirty-five," I all but shouted.

She put a hand on my knee. "I'm sorry."

"He was fine," I whispered.

When I'd carried him from that townhouse, he'd been in bad shape. Life-threatening shape. But he'd pulled through it.

He was dead.

"They'll have more details about arrangements tomorrow."

Dread filled every crevice within me.

"Will you stay? Go with me?" I sounded like a little boy begging, but if anyone understood my hate of funerals, it was Beau.

"Yeah. I'll stay."

I couldn't stand the worry on her face, especially knowing it was because of me.

"I'll be fine." There was no other choice. That didn't mean it would be easy. Cassano made some terrible choices in that fire, and ultimately, the ceiling would've collapsed no matter what we'd done. It still felt like I bore sole responsibility for his death, even though I knew full well accidents were an everyday part of the job.

"This isn't your fault." Her tone was stern, like she wanted to shake some sense into me.

"I'm gonna hit the hay." I stretched my arms above my head and faked a yawn.

"Teague . . ."

"I've been up since four and get to do it all over again tomorrow." I would've stood up for emphasis but didn't want to knock my sister off the arm.

"Why didn't you bunk at the firehouse?" Her gaze narrowed.

For someone who wasn't around much, she sure knew a whole lot about how my schedule worked. I guessed I'd mentioned it in passing when we talked that I slept at the fire station a lot.

"Captain cut my hours. Lucky me, I get to sleep in a comfortable bed." I meant that. Especially tonight. I couldn't handle being around the guys. I needed to process . . . without all the prying eyes.

"Need me to wake you up in the morning?"

"I'll set an alarm." I pointed to my phone.

Instead of getting up, Beau clamped down on my leg. "Don't let this eat at you. He wouldn't want that."

I remained still. No way would I make a promise I wasn't sure I could keep.

———

THREE HOURS LATER, I hadn't moved from the chair.

My mind spun out of control. The fire. The collapse. The heat. The weight.

Had I done the right thing insisting we stay together that night? If I'd let him go upstairs alone, would he have avoided the collapsed floor or gone down with it?

The only way for certain Cassano would still be alive was if that fire had never happened . . . or we'd stayed outside.

But that wasn't what we'd committed to do.

And I wouldn't have found Ash. Or Pepper.

Was Ash okay? Giving her my scarf seemed like a cop-out. I should be there for her . . . for all of them.

Pepper had so much responsibility on her hands.

And I needed her too.

I spun my phone in my hand. It was after eleven. I shouldn't wake her. Shouldn't risk Grey Paws.

Once again, my father had taken away something else I could control in my life. I could be there for Ash, for Pepper. She could use the help. *I* wanted to be the one to do that for her.

Instead, I'd made a mess of things.

My father would continue to have control as long as I let him.

I rose, stiff from sitting so long. Sleep wasn't coming, but a shower would be nice.

I tossed my phone on the bathroom counter. As I hung a towel on the rack, the phone mounted on the wall by the toilet was like a beacon.

How many times had I made fun of my brother for putting telephones in the bathrooms?

I closed the lid on the toilet, looked up the number to Grey Paws, and blocked the caller ID before I dialed.

Riiing.

It was late.

Riiing.

This was rude.

Riiing.

They're probably asleep.

Riiing.

I bet I woke the dogs.

Riiing.

"Hello?" A breathless sounding Pepper finally answered.

Relief rushed through me. I'd just seen her a few hours ago, but it was so good to hear her voice.

"Hey. Did I wake you?"

"No." A rustling came from the other end. "I just got back from walking Muffy and Sadie."

I sat up. "This late?"

"It takes a lot of time."

That didn't mean I had to like it. "It's dangerous."

"They need more exercise than I give them as it is," she snapped. "I can't help that I can't get it done within safe hours."

I should be there for her. It would cut the load in half, maybe more because Miss Adeline did a lot. But it wasn't good for her to be out in the cold late at night.

"You're doing a great job."

If I were there, she'd probably give me a dirty look for that comment, even if it was true.

"So great that I'm not one hundred percent sure everyone was fed. I was washing bowls and filling them at the same time." She sighed and I pictured her sinking into the chair behind the reception desk. "It was a disaster." Then she giggled. "But they all bark like they haven't eaten in a week."

On a night when I thought it impossible, my face cracked into a smile. "They'll take seconds and thirds, right?"

"Without a doubt."

"How's Ash?" I hoped she was one of the ones thrilled with more food.

"She's asleep with your scarf." There was a fondness in her voice.

A spark of jealousy flared that she could be there to see that and I couldn't. "I'm glad she's resting." And I was. That little bit of knowledge relaxed me a fraction.

"I thought about asking if you'd like to foster her since she has such an attachment to you." Foster? I—I hadn't had a dog since I was a kid. "But it's not a good idea."

Why? Did she think I wouldn't be good to Ash? Had the time I'd spent with them proven I wasn't fit to care for a dog?

That stung.

Regardless of what she thought, I wasn't in a position to have a pet. I spent more time at the fire station than at home. It simply wasn't feasible.

But knowing she thought so little of me . . . was disappointing.

"It wouldn't be fair to her," Pepper said quietly. "She's already so attached. If she spent more time with you only to be taken away later . . . she's been through enough already."

I slumped against the back of the toilet.

I don't want anyone else to have her.

That was possibly the most selfish thought I'd ever had. Ash deserved a home with more love than she could stand. But the idea I might never see her again didn't settle well. We had a connection, one that transcended explanation.

"You're right." The words sounded like they'd been dragged from me.

"I have to put them first." *Creak*. Had she finally sat down? "It has nothing to do with you."

That made me feel marginally better. I shifted. Why were toilets so hard and uncomfortable?

I stretched out my legs, but that didn't help my ass.

"Why are you making strange noises?"

I found myself smiling once again. "I'm using the phone in my brother's bathroom. The only place to sit is the toilet. And it's like a sheet of concrete."

She snickered. A little more of my tension eased.

"You could try the floor."

"It's marble. Or something even harder," I grumbled.

A comfortable silence stretched between us for a few moments. I'd temporarily forgotten the pile of crap that constantly weighed me down. Because she'd reminded me of the good.

"Why'd you call?" Only genuine curiosity laced the question.

I swallowed hard as the reason came crashing back.

"Cassano, he was the other firefighter at the blaze where I found Ash. The injured one. He—he died tonight."

"Teague," she breathed. "I'm—Are you okay?"

She'd almost said she was sorry. I knew it. And I was so grateful she hadn't. While I didn't doubt that she was, sometimes those words felt empty. What did it say about her that she was sensitive to that? That her immediate concern was me.

"I'm holding up." I picked at a string on the hand towel lying on the counter.

"It's hard to lose someone." The sadness in her tone spoke of experience.

"I know." All too well.

Cassano wasn't the first brother-in-arms I'd lost and he wouldn't be the last. I'd lost my mother. And in a way, I'd lost my father too.

But who had Pepper lost?

More silence.

What was there to say about Cassano? He was gone and nothing would bring him back. I hadn't done enough to save him.

"I'm going to try to get Ash to eat for a few days. I don't want to teach her bad habits. But if she won't, is it okay if Miss Adeline contacts you again?" Pepper asked tentatively.

"I'd rather hear from you," I blurted before I thought better of it.

"I'm not sure that's the best idea."

I liked the old woman, but she wasn't Pepper. And why did she have to be so wise?

"Whatever you need, I'm here." We'd just have to figure out a way to lay low.

She yawned. "I better go."

"Thanks." She'd been there for me when I needed to hear a friendly voice even though I didn't deserve it.

There was a long pause.

"Goodbye, Teague."

Before I could respond, there was a click. She was gone.

I hoped she got the rest she needed. That some of her worries would evaporate.

Just because you can't see her, doesn't mean you can't be there.

My sister's words came back to me in a flood.

Pepper needed more hands but would never ask for them. I could. I wanted to be there for her to support her, because that was where it felt right for me to be. By her side. With the dogs. Caring for them. Caring for Pepper. I wanted to be there with Pepper. Just . . . with her. Damn, I hated my father.

I grabbed my phone, not caring how late it was. After a few seconds scrolling, I found the number I was looking for and punched the call button.

"This better be good," the gruff voice answered.

He sounded awake. And the good news was, it was difficult to tell when he was in a good mood or a bad one. His demeanor was mostly the same.

"I need a favor."

CHAPTER TWENTY-EIGHT

PEPPER

"HELLO? ANYBODY HOME?"

I nearly tripped down the stairs when Muffy got under my feet. Luckily, I gripped the railing before I took a nosedive face first to the bottom.

"I told you we should've called," another voice said.

Was that—

"Hey. What are you two doing here?" It was seven thirty. I'd overslept. Sadie and Miss Adeline arguing downstairs had woken me up.

"We had a day off and thought we'd come hang out with you." Vivian flashed a cheeky grin at me.

Her best friend, Muriella, elbowed her in the side.

I was pretty sure Vivian didn't work. At least not a nine to five. She didn't have to. But Muriella was a teacher's aide a few days a week. Though I was fairly certain she didn't need to work either.

"Thank goodness you're not here about the fundraiser." I pretended to wipe sweat off my brow.

"We will need to discuss that at some point soon since it's five weeks away." Vivian hooked her arm through Muriella's. "We didn't bother taking our coats off. I've been told I should take exercise."

I rubbed my face. Clearly, I wasn't awake yet because my head was already spinning.

"Take exercise?" I asked carefully, unsure I wanted the answer.

Vivian waved me off. "Just a figure of speech. M and I are ready to walk some dogs." She tilted her head. "Unless we need to clean kennels."

Muriella smiled softly. "What she's trying to say is we're here to do whatever you need. Just put us to work."

I stared at them like they'd just beamed in from another planet. Yesterday, Miss Adeline and I had worked ourselves silly doing just the basic necessities. Now, like a miracle, help was here.

"Thank you." I motioned in a *come with me* gesture. "Umm . . . let's see what's going on in the chaos. Then we can figure out what needs to be done first."

"Dark Lady," one of Cher's hits, played from the radio. Miss Adeline sang and clapped along. When she caught us watching, she grinned.

Guessed I wasn't the only one with Teague on the brain. The reminder was a little painful, especially given the strange phone call last night. I'd wondered if I'd ever see him again as he left the park. Then, he'd called.

Because he lost a friend. One he thought he'd saved. He sounded so desperate, in so much pain. I wished more than anything I could have been with him, but I knew that wasn't possible. I knew what loss felt like.

"Are you going to stand there and stare or do something?" Miss Adeline's eyes were light as they bored into me.

"You have it under control." I turned to Vivian and Muriella. "Ladies, we can put our feet up and drink sangria."

"I knew we forgot to bring something." Vivian snapped her finger in front of her in a *dang it* move.

"Then I suppose we'll have to chip in." I slung an arm around Miss Adeline's shoulders. "Who's had breakfast?"

She pointed to the far end of kennels. "They have. And Sadie."

Of course Sadie had.

"If you're serious about walking them, I'll grab leads. But if it's too cold . . ."

"Not at all."

The bell jangled over the front door. We hadn't had this many visitors in forever.

As I took a step toward the lobby to see who was here—and why the door was unlocked—two familiar faces appeared.

"Told you we should've taken the subway," Vivian said.

One of the men scowled. The other grinned.

"But drivin' my truck around this town is so much fun," he said good-naturedly. "It's the parking that's a problem." He moved behind Muriella and wrapped his arms around her.

"Did you find a spot?" she asked.

He kissed the side of her temple. A pinch of jealousy nipped at my heart. Their affection was easy. The love radiated from them.

I'd never really thought about a partner until Teague barged into my world. Now it seemed he had one foot in and one foot out, which was worse than if he'd never been there at all.

Vivian patted her husband's cheek. "Someday you'll learn we're always right, and you're always wrong."

Daniel Elliott grunted and tucked a piece of hair behind her ear.

"Well, this is a surprise. Four of our favorite people, in the flesh." Miss Adeline raised the dog food scoop she held. "Why have you been such strangers?"

"Because Stone and M have a seven-month-old," Vivian said.

"And she's been pretending like she was the one pregnant," Muriella volunteered.

She shrugged. "It worked. I got waited on hand and foot."

"You always do, Princess," Daniel growled.

He was scary, all business all the time, but had been incredibly kind to us.

"Did you pray for volunteers?" I whispered to Miss Adeline.

She appeared as baffled by these four showing up as I was.

I scooped up a few leads off the counter. "I try to walk to the park and let them wander around for a while."

Except I hadn't been able to do that much since the arrival of our new friends. We'd make it to the park, but there wasn't time to let them just be dogs there. *I'd* been getting more exercise than any of them.

Millie let me slip the loop of the leash around her neck. I passed her off to Vivian. She bucked toward the door, ready to take off.

"I think we'll just do one at a time," I said.

"I can handle another puppy," Vivian said, even as Millie inched her closer to the door with her sheer strength.

"That's okay."

I leashed another dog and handed him to Daniel. In no time, they had four excited dogs stamping their feet in anticipation.

I loved that sound.

"Call me if you need me." I waved my cell phone.

They disappeared out the front door. Millie yanked Vivian ahead of the group and the sound of their laughter could be heard through the windows.

I wandered into the back.

"I'm not complaining, but what brought them to our doorstep?" She scooped the gourmet dog food in a bowl.

I lifted both shoulders and lowered them. "I honestly have no idea. I haven't talked to Vivian or Muriella in . . . a while." The days all ran together and I couldn't keep them straight.

"They came in the nick of time." She wiped under my eyes with her thumb. "You've got bags. And it's not from being ancient like me."

As soon as she filled a bowl, I put it in a kennel. The sweet smacking commenced before I could set the food down.

"In case you haven't noticed, the last few days have been stressful." I fell into work beside her.

"I noticed those dark circles under your eyes too."

I hadn't looked in a mirror except to brush my hair . . . and I hadn't spent more than a few seconds on that. And makeup? I didn't even know where mine was.

"You don't like my new look? Zombie extraordinaire?"

Muffy jumped up and down as I set his food on the floor. He gobbled half of it before I closed his kennel door.

"I didn't realize it was intentional." She scrunched her face up. "In that case, you've nailed it."

I held up my hand to high-five, and she shook her head.

"Have you noticed since Mr. October—"

The bell jangled over the front door, cutting off Miss Adeline . . . thankfully. I didn't particularly want to talk about Teague. All the mixed signals had me off balance. I still hadn't figured out what I wanted his signal to be exactly.

Bark. Bark. Bark.

"I'd better go make sure all the dogs and people are in one piece."

A man in a suit with a clipboard stood just inside the door. His gaze scanned the kennels lining the reception area like a robot doing inventory.

"Can I help you?" I asked in a raised voice over the barking.

He scowled. "Inspector Dawson from the Department of Agriculture and Markets."

That icky, nervous feeling that always attached itself to surprise visits squeezed my chest.

I fashioned a smile on my face, though it felt plastic. "Where's Inspector Smith? She usually drops in." *In the summer.* But why bother pointing that out?

"I need your business license and the record of the animals in your care for the past year."

Ba-dum. Ba-dum.

My heartbeat drummed in my ears. I hadn't had time to enter the Jersey track dogs into our system.

"Sure," I croaked.

He'd already moved over to the kennel closest to the door. He scribbled something on his notepad. Argh. Inspector Smith wasn't exactly going to win any personality contests, but at least she waited more than three seconds to make notes and demands.

Did they train these people to scare the crap out of us?

I walked into the back on shaky legs.

"What's wrong?" Miss Adeline asked, on high alert.

"State agriculture department is here."

"Inspector Smith?"

I shook my head. "He wants our record of the dogs," I whisper-hissed.

She looked to the side and winced. "Damn."

The small miracle I'd prayed for that maybe *she* had filled in the log evaporated.

"What are we going to do?"

She straightened. "You start working on it. I'll distract him."

"The book is in the desk." I pointed toward the reception area. "Out there."

She tiptoed to the door and peeked. Then she motioned me forward. "He has his back turned."

I crept to the desk. And held my breath as I kept my eyes glued to him.

Carefully, I pulled on the drawer.

Creeeaaak.

He whipped around. I flashed him a sheepish smile.

After another scowl, he returned to his work. I exhaled audibly, grabbed the log book, and practically ran to the back.

I rifled through a drawer until I found a pen. Miss Adeline kept watch, stealthily waiting for the right time to distract.

Oh crap.

I hadn't even added Ash to our records. The last entry was Oscar. I wracked my brain, trying desperately to remember if he was the dog we'd taken in before her.

I wasn't sure. But there was no time to waste.

I wrote as furiously as I could, certain we were going to get written up for this.

How much is the fine for an out-of-date book?

This was a violation Inspector Smith would allow us to correct. With this guy, we probably already had so many he'd need a ream of paper to print them all out.

Focus, Pepper.

I ran through my mental catalog for each new dog and checked what I'd written. That was all of them . . . I was pretty sure.

He appeared in the doorway and made a disgruntled noise as he took in more dogs. Sadie barked her head off as he approached her kennel.

But the acute sound of his pencil rubbing on the paper was loud and clear.

Once he moved down the row of kennels, I discreetly dropped treats into Sadie's. Her barks turned into smacking . . . until she finished her biscuit. *Woof. Woof.* The smarty pants barked again. I fed her another treat and wished this man would hurry up and finish before I had to give her the whole tin.

Miss Adeline widened her eyes at me. The woman knew when to speak and when to be quiet. She hadn't said a word to the man.

"Your papers?" he asked when he'd finished perusing—okay, more like scrutinizing.

I jumped. "Here's the log."

Sadie barked the second I stepped away. Even Inspector Dawson's nasty look didn't quiet her. If anything, it amped her up.

"The business license?" He sounded beyond unimpressed that I hadn't collected everything in a timely manner.

"I thought I'd picked it up." I pulled on one strap of my overall in a nervous fidget. "Let me grab it."

Once I set it in front of him, he barely glanced at the document. "This facility is only authorized to safely house eight dogs." What? Where did it say that on any paperwork we had from the city and state? Inspector Smith never mentioned it. And we *always* had more than eight dogs.

Miss Adeline opened her mouth, but I held up a hand.

"Please show me—"

"You have forty-eight hours to rectify the situation." He narrowed his gaze on me. "And I'm being generous. If I come back and there are nine dogs, I'm shutting you down."

CHAPTER TWENTY-NINE

PEPPER

"GIVE ME HIS CARD."

My hands trembled as I pulled the cardboard square from my pocket and handed it to Daniel.

I slumped against the counter, where I'd been since Inspector Dawson left, along with his list of violations.

I glanced to Miss Adeline in a *what are we going to do* look. She'd resumed feeding the dogs, though her movements were stilted and aggressive.

"I'm sorry we weren't here." Muriella placed a comforting hand on my shoulder.

"We can't adopt out that many dogs in two days," I said more to myself than anyone else.

Miss Adeline grunted. She still hadn't spoken. When she was quiet for this long, it was a little scary. Except I was already terrified.

"Did we mention we have a lot of space?" Vivian's voice was full of determination. "That jerk wants to play? Then let's play."

How did we go up against power? We couldn't afford an attorney and even if we could, there wasn't enough time.

All the innocent faces in those kennels . . . they were depending on us to protect them. If we were shut down, they'd take the dogs. Visions of them in the overcrowded city shelter bleached my brain.

They did the best they could. We'd taken dogs off their hands before.

But they killed.

I white-knuckled the edge of the counter.

Nausea rolled through my stomach in a wave.

An arm slipped around my waist. I leaned my head on Miss Adeline's shoulder.

"We always figure it out, don't we?" she whispered.

I nodded.

"We can take them today, but since they're comfortable here, it might be best to do it tomorrow," Vivian said. "They can stay until we get the jerk-face off your back."

"Take them?" My brain was foggy with nightmare scenarios to the point I couldn't think.

"Did you not hear me?" she asked. "I said we have plenty of space."

"We can't ask you to do that," I said quietly. "If we get caught—"

"What are they going to do to us?" Vivian looked smugly at her husband, whose back was toward us as he spoke low into his phone.

"Take them all. Shut us down permanently." I was going to be sick.

Sadie pawed at her cage like she was trying to dig out. I opened it and sank to my knees. She bolted straight into me, covering my face with kisses. I couldn't lose them. They were my life.

"He's legit," Daniel said as he strode back in the room. "And he has the authority to do what he said, even though it wasn't precedent with previous inspectors."

"We've solved the problem," Vivian said. Daniel looked warily at his wife. "They'll come hang out with us until this blows over."

What if it didn't blow over? I was beyond grateful for their help, but it wasn't a permanent solution.

"They can't just disappear. We'll have to show who took possession of the dogs," I said. Hiding them out wouldn't be good enough.

"You can put them all in my name." Stone tugged on his ball cap.

He was a massive movie star—at least he had been before he quit—but he'd always been down-to-earth and kind.

"That won't do. We can't turn over that many dogs to one person." As much as I wanted to take him up on the offer, it wouldn't work.

"They try to be asses and I'll take it public. Besides, we've got a lot of acres in Texas. More than enough for the dogs. If they ask questions, our alibi is airtight." His stance was casual, easy, like he'd solved all the problems.

Had he?

"Not to mention we're having the adoption event soon," Muriella said.

I put my head to Sadie's and rubbed behind her ears. The adoption event. I—I couldn't get excited about it. As crazy as this girl drove me, I didn't want to let her go. We were her forever home.

And she wasn't the only one.

I never should've agreed to the event in the first place. Maybe that was selfish. Maybe I needed an attitude adjustment. A new way of thinking.

But as Muffy nudged his door and wagged his tail, I knew we did something right.

As many dogs as we had at the rescue, they were happy.

I'd always be proud of that.

"We're not letting some old mean man stop us, are we?" I whispered to Sadie.

I drew in a long breath and let it out slowly. When I rose to my feet, I looked around at the supportive faces. Thank goodness they were here.

"Are you sure you want to do this?" I asked. Miss Adeline gave me an approving nod.

"We *are* doing this," Muriella said.

"Thank you." A lump formed in my throat but I quickly swallowed it down. "We have a few who are recovering from injuries, so they'll stay here." I rubbed Sadie's head. "Along with the troublemakers."

Woof.

At least she didn't deny who she was. *See?* Greyhounds spoke English.

"If either Miss Adeline or I can come take a look at where you think you can keep them, we can get you the supplies you need." With every word, optimism infused me. "And of course, they won't be solely your responsibility. We'll come care for them."

"I'll have the furniture removed from the living room. That should be plenty of space for everyone."

All eyes jerked to Daniel. His expression remained cool and calm.

Then Vivian kissed his cheek. "I like that solution."

Stone slung an arm around Muriella's shoulders and grabbed a leash off the counter behind them. "We better get back to it. I'm thinking you need more help than us walking four dogs."

It was hard to admit the truth. I liked taking care of things myself, and for such a long time, that was exactly what I had been doing. With Miss Adeline, of course. But in the past few weeks, it had felt like an army had entered my life, slowly showing me I was wrong. That it was okay to say "yes, please" and "thank you" when help was offered. And one of those times was now.

CHAPTER THIRTY

TEAGUE

"YO!"

I stirred the chili simmering on the stove, not in the mood for Burke.

He clapped my shoulder. "How much longer?"

I'd come in early for my shift to cook. Actually, it was to avoid being alone with my thoughts for a minute more. I couldn't turn off the images of the fire that had ultimately taken Cassano's life. It didn't seem possible he was dead.

"About ten minutes." My answer was robotic. I didn't sound like myself. Didn't *feel* like myself.

I'd hoped being at the firehouse would bring a sense of normalcy back.

It hadn't.

"I'll go tell the fellas." He snorted. "It'll take that long to get them to the table." Burke was behaving almost like himself. But there was something off. His joke not quite authentic. Like he was overdoing it.

Because we'd lost a brother.

I continued stirring on autopilot.

"Shit." I banged the spoon on the side of the pot before I stirred it too much.

My phone chimed.

Call me.

I put the lid back on the pot of chili and turned around one of the kitchen chairs. As I hit Daniel's name on my phone, I sat backward in the chair.

"An inspector paid a visit to Grey Paws today."

No.

Just when I thought things couldn't get worse. And this was completely my fault.

"What happened?" I spat.

"They have to get down to eight dogs in forty-eight hours or they're shut down."

"Son of a . . ." I stood, the chair scraping across the linoleum when I did. I kicked it. There was no satisfaction when it fell on its side.

"I've called my contacts, but I don't think we can stop this."

We couldn't stop it. *I* could.

Daniel was a powerful man in the city. His reach was far and wide in ways I didn't really want to know the source of.

But my father was more powerful. Had more money. Played dirty to get what he wanted.

Unstoppable.

He was a force no one could contain.

No. One.

"Find anything you can on that man. Get him demoted, moved . . . anything." The desperate quality to my voice was one I didn't recognize.

"Already on it." He paused. "We're helping Pepper and Miss Adeline. I just thought you'd want to know what was going on."

"I want to know everything."

I ended the call, picked up the overturned chair, and turned off the stove.

"It's ready." I shouldered past Walsh and Rivera as I stormed out of the kitchen.

If I hadn't seen Pepper yesterday, would my father have sent his goon to torment her? If I'd showed up for duty at Hollingsworth Properties, would that have stopped him? There was no way to know.

"Where the hell are you going? You're on in a half hour," Captain called as I shoved out the back door.

"Family emergency," I grunted.

When I reached my truck, I yanked open the door and climbed inside. Instead of starting it, I sagged against the steering wheel.

Where was I going?

If I went to Grey Paws, a fresh hell would be rained down on Pepper.

My breath came in short, heavy pants. I couldn't catch it.

How could I fix this for her? What would happen to the dogs? Who would care for them like they did?

Without thought, I dialed.

"Are you at work?" Just hearing my brother's voice allowed me to take a deeper breath.

"He's going to shut her down," I croaked. "How do I stop it?"

A tense silence floated between us.

"By being smart. Whatever you're thinking of doing, wait."

He knew me better than anyone. Somehow I'd tamped down my urge to go to Pepper . . . but I had a few other people I wanted to pay a visit to. Starting with that inspector.

"Daniel's helping her. But it should be me." My voice crescendoed to a shout.

"If you get near her, it's only going to hurt Pepper."

I resented it but was relieved my brother had the ability to remain calm in the midst of turmoil.

"I got her into this mess. I need to get her out."

"He did this. Not you." Lincoln was as fierce as I'd ever heard him. "Do you understand me?"

Loud and clear. But that didn't mean I agreed with him.

"Go to work. Get your head on straight. We'll figure this out as a family."

He was right. I was in no frame of mind to do anything other than the job that was second-nature. Even that was going to be hard.

"All right." I put my hand on the door handle.

"We'll come up with something."

I nodded, despite he couldn't see me. "You still at the office?" It was late afternoon and a stupid question. He was always working.

"No. I just finished up a meeting with Dad and I'm headed out to look at some property."

Maybe he did get out of that prison every so often.

"I won't be home until late."

After I hung up, I sat there with one hand on the door handle and the other on the steering wheel. Lincoln had a way of settling my temper. He was solid, had reasonable wisdom. He was always there for me, no matter what.

I cranked my truck.

And this time, I ignored his advice.

CHAPTER THIRTY-ONE

TEAGUE

"SIR. HE'S NOT HERE."

For the second time in a week, my father's receptionist chased after me. I'd believe her when I saw with my own eyes.

On the drive over, I still hadn't decided what I was going to do once I confronted him. Part of me wanted to give in, do what he wanted, and pray he kept his word he'd leave Grey Paws alone. Except I couldn't recall him saying exactly those words.

In my father's world, promises were meant to be broken.

I shoved one of the mahogany double doors to his office.

And found the receptionist had spoken the truth.

He wasn't there.

When I spun to retreat, she flashed an *I told you so* look in my direction. I ignored her and marched back toward the lobby.

Now what?

My grand plan failed.

"Don't you want to know where he is?" Her tone was a taunt.

I hesitated at the elevator. Did I? I wasn't much for signs, but maybe this had been one that my brother was right.

Without answering, I stabbed the down button. Mercifully, the elevator arrived quickly.

"Should I tell Mr. Hollingsworth you dropped by?" She smirked and finger waved as the doors closed.

She'd tell him, no matter what I said.

I leaned against the wall. Should I go back to work? Or go to Pepper?

The pull was strong in her direction. She already had enough to deal with before I came into the picture. I hated to be uncertain. But I truly didn't know if it would do her more harm than good if I went to help her.

Damned if I do, and damned if I don't.

As I wheeled out of the parking garage onto East Fifty-sixth Street, I glanced behind me. A black car eased away from the curb into traffic. It looked eerily similar to the one I'd seen at the fire yesterday.

I checked the rearview mirror every few seconds. The car maintained a safe distance behind me.

I turned.

It turned.

I pulled over.

It pulled over.

Once again, my father made the decision for me. I cruised back to the firehouse. I was only an hour late for my shift.

One question pounded in my brain.

Why did he care what I did?

It couldn't simply be power or control. If he'd wanted a relationship with me, he'd had more than enough opportunities to repair that over the years. Up until this point, I'd have been willing to hear him out if he'd have shown any sign of remorse.

I'd be wary. But willing.

No longer.

I didn't bother with a turn signal when I hung a left into the lot behind the fire station. The car rolled past as if it were any ordinary vehicle.

Was he in there?

Had he known I'd come to him? Shit. What if he thought Pepper had told me about the inspector?

I parked, grabbed my phone, and fired off a text.

Can you keep eyes on GP?

Daniel responded in seconds.

Already on it.

I sagged in relief. At least someone would be there to watch over them, even if it couldn't be me.

I killed the engine and opened the door.

Buzz. Buzz. Buzz.

I checked the incoming call and did a double take. Cassano's name splashed across the screen.

My finger shook as I swiped to answer.

"Teague? It's Ellen Cassano."

I dropped my head back until it hit the headrest.

"Hey." Guilt harpooned me in the chest. Why hadn't I already called his wife to offer my condolences? Because I'd been too consumed with myself.

"I wanted to let you know"—sniffles fired through the phone at me —"the funeral is tomorrow," she choked out.

A solid lump formed in the back of my throat. "I'll be there."

There was a pause, neither of us able to speak.

"Thank you." She'd somehow managed to compose herself, and I was wowed by her strength. "I'd like you to be a pallbearer. Freeman thought the world of you. And you saved him from that fire."

But he was still dead.

I couldn't find the words to answer. She'd gone out of her way to ask me to do a great honor. If it weren't for me, her husband might still be alive.

"Will you, Teague? He'd have wanted you to."

I cleared my throat. "Yeah." It was a pitiful response, but the best I could come up with. "I'm so sorry, Ellen."

More sniffles. "Me too. I'll see you tomorrow."

I closed my eyes as I dropped the phone on the seat beside me. The blows just kept on coming. I missed him too. It seemed impossible he was gone. I understood what it was like to lose someone, but I'd been too young to have to deal with the arrangements.

What strength Ellen had.

My mind drifted back to the days after my mother died. Had it been hard on my father? I honestly couldn't remember anything but his blank expression at the funeral.

I dreaded tomorrow.

Which was completely unfair. I owed it to Cassano to pay my respects, but I hated funerals and all the memories they brought back. All the uncontrollable emotions. I'd learned to wrangle them on a daily basis, though they came at me no matter what.

At least Beau would be there.

Tap. Tap. Tap.

Burke's face pressed against the window. I jumped, beyond startled, and flipped him the bird. He laughed.

"Thought you had a family emergency?" he asked as I opened the door into him.

"Wasn't what I thought," I said gruffly. It was worse, but I needed to take my brother's advice and not do anything to push our father into a frenzy.

"Captain was so pissed when you left, he was muttering to himself."

I scowled. That wasn't good. I clapped Burke on the back. "Here's hoping I don't get suspended again." I faked being at ease.

"How many you got left?" He shoved me.

I stumbled and flipped him off again. "Pretty sure I'm about out."

CHAPTER THIRTY-TWO

PEPPER

"UMM, WOW."

The second we'd gotten on the elevator of Daniel and Vivian's apartment building, I'd tried not to touch anything. It was posh and . . . I was far from it.

But when I stepped into their penthouse, it was like being transported to another world. Even in movies, I'd never seen anything like this.

The living room had no furniture, just as he'd promised only a couple hours ago. Floor-to-ceiling windows provided a view of the city that was breathtaking.

Vivian elbowed me in the side. "I felt the same way the first time I saw it."

They were so down-to-earth. Well, Daniel was a little scary, but they were good people.

But even in the grandeur of the apartment, something odd stuck out to me. It felt like a home.

"What do you think?" Muriella asked, gesturing to the open space. "If it's not big enough, we have the floor below and our family also has several apartments in the building."

Not big enough? The entire rescue could fit in this room.

I put my hands behind my back and took a tentative step forward. I didn't want to dirty anything. "Should I take off my shoes?"

"If it'll make you feel more at home." Vivian linked her arm through mine and dragged me farther into the room. "Will this work?"

I looked around at all of them. These people were normally the picture of confidence, but they all seemed to be anxious to hear my verdict. Like they truly cared if I approved of this space for the dogs.

"It's . . ." Vivian leaned in while I tried to find adequate words. "Fantastic." So that wasn't the most articulate, nevertheless it was the truth.

She relaxed against me. "Think they'll like the window?"

"They'll love it. I just hope you have a lot of glass cleaner." I tried to contain my excitement. This was just a temporary home until we could get that inspector off our backs, but it was a relief knowing we wouldn't have to be hiding the dogs in closets or cars or wherever we could find.

"My grandmama made me clean windows every Saturday," Stone said. "I'm great at it."

"Good to know." I laughed before I walked along the perimeter. "If you're okay with having them loose in this area, we have enough beds to set up here." I motioned toward the wide opening between the living room and foyer. "I think we have enough gates to partition this off." I glanced down. "I am concerned about the floor. These hardwoods and dog nails . . ."

"Do they like rugs?"

Once again, Daniel caught me off guard with his question. For such a closed-off man, he seemed to catalog everything.

"That would be okay. I'd be more comfortable if we could preserve the integrity of the floor," I said.

Vivian dragged me down the hall that forked off from the foyer and living room. She flipped a light switch when we were halfway down it and pointed at the floor. "Does this look like we're worried about puppy writing on the floor?"

There was a long gash in the hardwood and another shorter one not too far away.

"No," I finally said. How had we gotten so lucky to have these people in our lives?

"If a rug is better for them, that's what we'll get. But don't you worry for one second about a few little dings."

I released a breath. "Thank you."

Daniel appeared at the end of the hallway. "We'll get everything set up tonight. Tomorrow we'll transport the dogs here."

I wouldn't be able to watch the dogs 24/7, but they'd be in loving hands.

I had Miss Adeline and the dogs. That was more than some people ever had. Family took all shapes and forms. I wouldn't trade mine for anything.

But it could grow.

"Make a list of everything we need to have here and what we need to do every day," Vivian said.

"Like you'll look at that." Muriella gave Vivian the side eye.

"It was for you. So you can tell me what I need to do," she shot back.

"I'll introduce you to Paul and you'll have access to the building any time you need it," Daniel interjected, apparently good at refereeing.

I nodded. "I hope we can get this situation sorted sooner rather than later. I'm sure you'll want your living room back."

"Pshh." Vivian flicked her hand down. "We never use it."

I shifted on my feet. "I should get back, but thank you."

"I'll give you a ride," Stone offered.

"No," I said quickly. "I appreciate it. I'm good though."

"Let me walk you out."

Arguing with Daniel was another story. His tone left no room for it.

"Thank you all again."

"We're happy to help. Don't be afraid to ask for what you need," Muriella said.

"Okay." I shoved my hands in the pockets of my overalls. "And I promise I won't let Miss Adeline come over here. If I do, you'll have a permanent houseguest." Although that could backfire. She'd love to be pampered just as much as I knew the dogs would be.

CHAPTER THIRTY-THREE

TEAGUE

I'M ONLY HERE *to get my suit.*

Then why was I creeping past Grey Paws instead of parking my truck and heading for my loft?

A few lights were on inside, despite the late hour. Pepper moved about with a leash over her shoulder. She was talking to someone, but I couldn't tell if it was Miss Adeline or one of the dogs.

Honk. Honk.

She looked out at the street when the car behind me blared its horn. They could stick it. Except I'd likely been busted. My truck wasn't exactly discreet.

She continued to look out the window. I crept by, only glancing at the street ahead to make sure I didn't hit one of the parked cars.

The horn blasted again.

I rolled down my window and motioned the driver around. They wheeled past with another honk and a one-finger salute. How kind of them to tell me I was number one.

Pepper remained fixed on me until I was past. Something about seeing her, even from afar, soothed me.

Despite the time, I found a parking spot a few blocks away. Just before I opened the door, I checked the rearview mirror. Headlights flicked off.

There hadn't been an open spot or I would've taken it. Were they in the street?

That black car I kept seeing and my father were making me paranoid.

I shook it off and hustled to my loft.

Except once I was inside, I didn't go upstairs to grab my clothes.

I strode straight out the back into the alley.

As I lifted a hand to knock on the door to Grey Paws, it swung open. I jumped out of the way.

Pepper let out a strangled cry and dropped the trash bag in her grasp.

"Sorry," I whispered.

"Teague?" She peered at me in the dim light of the alley. "What are you doing here? You scared me to death."

"I—" I plowed my fingers through my hair. "I don't know what I'm doing here." *Besides tempting trouble.*

She looked around again. "Where's your truck?"

"Out there." I motioned to the building like it was an up and over gesture.

I took the trash bag handle from her and hefted it into the nearby dumpster.

She remained blocking the entrance as she propped the door open. *Was she keeping me out? Was that why I wanted in so much?*

"Hey, you don't have on a jacket." I shrugged mine off my shoulders.

She backed inside. "I'm letting all the heat out."

The opening shrank, but she didn't close the door in my face.

I stuck my foot out to keep it from clicking shut, and she held it open.

A shrill bark rang out.

And it wasn't Sadie bossing everyone around.

Ash was on her feet, digging at the bottom of her kennel door to get to me. I strode over and crouched. She licked my fingers through the gate.

"May I?" I touched the latch.

Pepper nodded. "She needs to go for a walk. And she might like a snack."

I pushed up the lever.

Ash sprinted out, tackling me to the floor. She licked at my face, my arm, my neck . . . anywhere she could reach.

All the other dogs checked to see what the commotion was about.

"Hey." I rubbed down her wiggling body. "How's my girl?"

She sat on my lap, even though she didn't fit, and swiped her big tongue over my cheek.

I laughed and wiped away the slobber. "That good, huh?"

She burrowed against me, her tail slapping my side.

"Have you been eating?"

"Better, but she didn't eat much dinner." Pepper leaned against the counter with her arms crossed. Her stress was palpable. I sensed the wall she'd erected around herself in the past couple of days.

But I got it.

She needed to block out her feelings so she could survive.

"Are you hungry?"

Ash licked my face again.

"Guess that's a yes." I laughed again. It occurred to me that for a minute, she'd helped me forget the crappy things happening all around me.

Pepper prepared a bowl of food and sat on the floor beside us. Ash gobbled it up before she handed the dish to me.

She shook her head. There was relief and worry in her expression all at once. "What if I can't get her to eat without you?"

"I won't let her starve." I didn't know how I'd make that happen, but I would.

She fiddled with the corduroy fabric on the leg of her overalls. I hated the heavy burden she seemed to carry and that I'd done anything to add to that weight.

"I heard about what happened." The apology was in my voice, but there weren't enough sorrys in the world to adequately convey just how much I was.

She snapped her head up. "Did Miss Adeline call you?"

"No." Part of me wondered if I was honest if I'd lose my source of information. "I've known Daniel a long time."

She narrowed her eyes as if staring at me would give her all the answers she was looking for. Pieces seemed to click into place. "Do you happen to know anything about why they showed up out of the blue?" She put air quotes around out of the blue.

"Were they helpful?" I was a little afraid if I answered yes what she might do . . . like kill me with her death glare.

"Did you ask them to keep the dogs?" Her words were hesitant, like she wasn't sure if she wanted to know the truth.

"No." If I'd have known the situation, I would've . . . or I'd have figured something else out.

She nodded, seemingly satisfied. "It's like they showed up at just the right moment."

I couldn't take total responsibility for that, but at least through them, I'd been there for her.

"It's okay to ask for help."

"I know that," she snapped, then sighed. "I'm sorry. I'm cranky to have to shuffle the dogs when they're finally getting settled."

I slung an arm around her shoulders and pulled her close. She leaned her head against mine. Ash rested in my lap.

A quiet contentment surrounded us despite all the chaos. It was a moment of peace . . . of hope that everything would be okay.

"I'm so scared." Her wretched whisper nearly broke me. "I can't lose them."

Ash licked Pepper's hand in support.

"You won't."

How could I say that with confidence? I had no idea what would happen. I'd do everything in my power to make sure she didn't, but what my father ordained always happened.

And I was a terrible person for letting my negativity steal the hope I should've projected.

"I trust Daniel and Vivian, but *I* should be the one looking after the dogs. We're already spread so thin. How am I going to do that when they're in two places?"

I closed my eyes, hating how torn apart she was. What was there to say? How could I make this right for her?

"They'll be in a penthouse for goodness sake, but I'm still worried." And that worry was carved into every single syllable she spoke. "They're my family."

Something in me snapped. Anger like I'd never known sliced through me in vicious streaks. She shouldn't have to be scared. She didn't deserve this fresh hell.

I wrapped my other arm around her and pulled her close. It was awkward. And I squeezed the life out of her. But I needed to comfort her.

"I've known Daniel and now Vivian for quite some time. And if there is one thing they do exceptionally well, it's rally around those they care for. And they don't do anything halfway. So, just know that they will be the ones bending over backwards to help you. They won't think of this as a burden. That's just the people they are. And I'm thinking that it will be okay if you let down your incredible work ethic for a moment and take the reprieve they're giving you." Just like I'm taking this moment as a reprieve from my screwed-up life.

"I'll try," she whispered. "I'll try."

After a minute, she relaxed against my chest. I kissed the top of her head. She slid her arms around my waist and held me as tight as I was holding her.

Eventually her labored breathing turned even. Her hold on me loosened as a soft snore escaped her. Ash looked up at me. Some sort of unspoken understanding passed between us. She wanted me to stay.

I nodded, and she too closed her eyes. As I looked around the space, I tried to remain still. Everyone was asleep.

I had no idea if anyone had been walked . . . or if I should risk waking Pepper by attempting to take everyone out.

They were quiet. Peaceful.

So I kept her in my embrace. Reveled at the feel of her in my arms.

She was warm. As much a comfort to me as I hoped I was to her. It was easy to see why she loved this place. Loved these animals.

She was doing good but not for the glory of it. Because it was right. It was her reason and purpose. She didn't have to utter those words to me. I *saw* it every single time I was with her.

I didn't have many heroes. Respect was something I didn't give easily.

But Pepper? Miss Adeline? What they did with fearlessness, no matter how tired they got?

I admired their tenacity and drive.

And if the best thing I could do was hold Pepper so she could get some rest, so be it.

Because this right here . . . I wanted to hang on to this moment for as long as I could.

CHAPTER THIRTY-FOUR

PEPPER

SNIFF. *Sniff. Sniff.*

Reluctantly, I opened my eyes as the familiar sound greeted me. Luminous gray eyes looked at me, a big dark nose working in overtime. *What is Ash doing out?*

What wasn't familiar was our bed.

My head was on one side and hers on the other of a broad chest. My arm was over a taut stomach, and her paw rested on an opposite ab.

I risked a glance up.

Teague.

The last thing I remembered was being burrowed into his comforting embrace. Now, we were sprawled on the floor, surrounded by dogs.

And my heart clenched.

Because he fit right into the place where I was most comfortable.

His chest rose and fell in a steady and sure rhythm. The worry lines on his face were smoothed away by sleep. Yet his arms were braced around me and Ash, protective even when he was asleep.

I didn't want to need him.

Dependency was a dangerous thing.

But I liked he was here.

Liked that instead of the weight of responsibility I normally woke up to, I felt inspired and ready to tackle the day.

Because I was rested.

Renewed.

And supported.

The pile of dogs lifted their heads in sync.

Miss Adeline stood in the doorway. I started to sit up, but she put a finger to her lips. My cheeks got hot at being caught in this position. Boy was I going to hear about this later.

Her gaze was mischievous, yet pleased in a way I wasn't sure I'd ever seen. She lifted a leash in a silent *I'll start walking the dogs* and grabbed her coat.

Sadie, tired of being ignored, barked. And barked. And barked.

Teague stirred.

I froze, uncertain if I should scramble away when all I really wanted to do was stay.

When his brown eyes locked on mine, I couldn't move. Through the haze of sleep there was an intensity I'd never seen before. But I *felt* it.

He seemed to be examining my every feature.

Oh crap. My hair was no doubt a disaster. I probably had crease lines in my face and maybe drool since I'd slept harder than I ever had in my life.

I touched the corner of my mouth. Nothing. *Thank goodness.*

Automatically, I dropped my hand back to his stomach. Amusement flickered in his gaze, yet that intensity remained.

"I didn't want to move you last night." His voice was deeper, roughened with sleep.

"This is my favorite place to sleep." The confession was out before I could stop it. Miss Adeline knew it. The dogs knew it. But no one else did.

Amusement turned to curiosity. "Hope that means you didn't mind no pillow or covers." Discreetly, he pulled me closer to him.

Except I was already glued to his side.

I liked his warmth. I liked the safety of his hold.

I like waking up to him.

Oh no. I could not be thinking crazy things like that.

He brushed his thumb over my temple. "Whatever is going on up there, just stop."

"Are you telling me how to think?" There was no bite to my words. My lips even tilted upward. And strangely enough, he *had* quieted my mind.

"I wouldn't dare. Just try not to overthink."

Ash licked him in the face in a sneak attack. He laughed and kissed the top of her head.

Bark. Bark. Bark.

He stuck his finger in his ear and winced. "Pretty sure that's our cue to get up."

He slid to a sitting position before getting to his feet.

I placed my hand in his and he easily lifted me to stand.

Neither of us moved, even as Sadie barked. That intensity was back with a vengeance. I just had no idea what it meant.

He squeezed my fingers and kissed the top of my head.

This man always got to me with the way he treated my dogs, but his simple affections were a double punch to the heart.

"Should I feed her? Before we all lose our hearing?" He grinned.

"Good idea."

I grabbed the food out of the refrigerator. He wiped out one of the clean bowls drying on the counter.

"This scoop in each bowl." I pushed the container toward him and set the measuring cup on top.

He set to work filling and I distributed. It was never like this. We'd had volunteers over the years, and occasionally, they'd helped with the feeding, walking, and even playing with the dogs. But this felt different. As if we were a team. In sync.

"The queen first," I said as Sadie jumped on me to get to her bowl. I snapped my fingers and pointed down. She ignored me and kept her big paws on my leg. Stubborn thing. "Fine. You win. Again."

Teague and I worked together like a well-oiled machine. Miss

Adeline popped in and took another dog out to walk. We were seamless. Didn't get in one another's way.

I could get used to this.

How many times had I thought that when he was around? It had been a slow battle to let Miss Adeline completely in. I'd never felt comfortable enough to be myself around anyone but the dogs. Maybe that was because they'd accepted me when I'd been at my worst. They'd never judged. They'd been genuinely happy to be around me.

Even if I couldn't pinpoint why Teague was different, every time I was around him, I became more aware that he was. My initial *stop! stay back!* reaction had been normal. I hadn't liked him. Yet even when he disappointed me, he still managed to redeem himself.

"Why do you keep coming back?" I blurted before I could think better of it. Seemed my subconscious determination to keep people away was still very much alive and active.

He hesitated mid-scoop but quickly continued. "I guess my father taught me one good thing. Don't ever give up."

I winced, hating I'd brought his father to the forefront of his mind. Obviously it was painful for him, though I wondered if the man wasn't always there anyway.

I tilted my head, considering the brief time we'd known one another. Only one time had I seen him seem to give up. But it hadn't taken him long to go back at it . . . with me at least. Maybe when he'd conceded to his father it wasn't really that at all.

"If you don't have much to do with him, how did he teach you that?" I became a sponge, eager to know whatever information I could glean about Teague.

He offered me a full bowl. "Growing up, he showed us that every single day." His face hardened. "Except with the most important thing."

My fingers trembled at the menace in his tone as I took the bowl. "What was that?"

His features were like granite, hatred etched into every facet of them. "Finding out who murdered my mother."

CHAPTER THIRTY-FIVE

TEAGUE

THE WORDS that shall not be spoken.

My mother's murder was a known fact. It had been covered by news organizations all over the world.

Yet in my family, it was no-go territory.

We could mention she was gone. But not the specifics.

Yet here I was airing personal business to a practical stranger.

Pepper gasped.

Judging by her reaction, she didn't know my mother was murdered. I'd wondered after my entire family had barged into her space if she'd looked us up. Dug deeper to find out who we were. Although, given how busy she was, would she have had time? Would she have bothered?

My father had done an excellent job of burying those old stories of my mother's death, but they were still out there.

She dropped the bowl and grasped my arms. "I'm so sorry." She looked down a minute, but when her gaze lifted back to mine, I'd never seen such earnestness. "I know that doesn't do any good, but I am."

Somehow her sorry meant something. Some of the ones I'd heard had been heartfelt, yet most had been hollow.

"I appreciate that." My voice was scratchy. "I should be past it by now. It was a long time ago—"

"You never have to get over it." The firmness of her tone as she shook me caught me by surprise.

No one had ever said that to me.

I'd been expected to move on. Pretend it hadn't happened.

Yet I lived with it every day. It never went away.

I didn't need her permission to feel whatever it was that I did, but having that acknowledgment loosened something inside of me.

"I was there." The whisper sounded as if it had been yanked from the depths where I'd buried it deep.

"Teague." Her fingers dug into my arms.

The memories that usually plagued my sleep flashed across my brain.

"I was five. She was loading me into the car after we'd stopped at our favorite deli."

Pepper disappeared from in front of me. I was back in the front seat of Mom's Cadillac.

"SHOULD *we set up a picnic for supper?" She grabbed my seatbelt and leaned over me.*

"Yes! Lincoln and Beau and Dad will love that." I pumped my fist in the air.

She laughed. "They will. Should we stop by Daddy's office and drag him home?"

"Can we?"

"We can." Click. "All safe now." She kissed my forehead. "Love you—"

Pop. Pop. Pop.

Her eyes went wide. "Teague," she whispered before she fell.

Her head landed in my lap.

"HE SHOT HER IN THE BACK."

The pain in my chest I always had when I woke up from that

nightmare flared to life. Except this time, this was no dream. It had happened in the day. When I was awake.

"I saw his face. But I—" I hung my head. I'd looked at picture after picture the police had presented me. Endured my father's agitation that none of them were who I saw. That I just couldn't remember other than the blurry image.

Her slender arms wrapped around me. She buried her head against my chest. Although she was cradled to me, it felt as if I were the one in her arms. That she was bigger and I was small.

It was the hug I'd needed from that horrific day. One I'd never gotten from my father and just wasn't the same from my brother or sister.

I sank into her embrace. The fog of the memory slowly evaporated until my head was clear. She hadn't bothered with words of support. She simply showed me.

I wouldn't forget that.

She pulled back quickly, despair and worry written on her face. "Your friend. You have the funeral . . ."

Pepper couldn't articulate what she was attempting to say, but I understood. She recognized that death and funerals had an impact on me beyond what a person might normally feel. Not that there was a normal.

Death was hard.

While it would have been easy to cast aside the idea that would be presented later today and that I'd heard countless times, that Cassano was in a better place, I chose not to. I couldn't.

It gave me some solace believing those I'd lost were somewhere better, even if I wished they were still here.

"My sister is going with me," I finally said. What would I have done if she were in London?

Pepper nodded, satisfied, though her mouth remained in a flat line. "I'm glad you have them."

"Me too." I shook off the cloud around us. The day was going to be difficult. I couldn't dwell on it. "Want some breakfast? I make a mean omelet."

Red crept up her cheeks. "I don't know if we have any eggs."

"Are you good to go down here?"

"I think it's under control . . . sort of." The flat line of her lips turned up.

"Mind if I go rummage in your kitchen?"

"Go for it. Though I can't promise Miss Adeline won't come get in your way." The affection in her voice every time she spoke of the woman was present again.

"She could probably show me a thing or two."

"I definitely could." The woman appeared with a smug look. "Looks like you could give a lesson in taking things at a snail's pace."

Pepper closed her eyes in embarrassment. "Woman . . ."

"I don't want to hear any excuses." She waved us off. "And I like my omelet extra done."

"Got it." I saluted.

She ambled away to take another dog out for a walk.

"Feel free to ignore her," Pepper said.

I tapped my lips. "I don't know. She may be onto something."

She shoved at me. "Not you too."

"Fine, fine. I'll go cook breakfast."

Bark. Bark. Bark.

"I thought you already fed her?" I asked over Sadie's shrill barks.

"You said the B word." She mouthed *breakfast* before she pointed in the dog's direction. "And you already ate, little piggy."

That only seemed to encourage her.

"Maybe she wants an omelet."

The girl stood there barking as if she wouldn't stop until her voice gave out. A few others joined the chorus.

Pepper shook her finger at Sadie. "See what you've started."

"Remind me not to make you mad." I held up both hands in surrender.

She planted a hand on her hip, but there was zero menace in her glare. *Damn, she's beautiful.*

After a second of my staring, she appeared uncertain. "What?"

"What what?"

"You're looking at me funny," she said, glancing down I guessed to check to see if she had something on her clothes.

"Not funny." I stalked toward her. "Not by a long shot."

And then she was in my arms, I'd hooked her by the waist, and pulled her flush. We hadn't known each other long, but I'd had a few moments when she'd been in my arms. Her skin was soft to touch. When I held her, it felt perfect. But right now, I needed to know if her sweet lips were as soft as they seemed.

I bent my head and found her lips with mine before I could over-think it. She blinked at me in surprise but didn't push me away.

Her mouth was soft, yet when she finally kissed me back, it was strong. She wove her fingers through my hair and held me in place. I cradled her face. That perfect pale skin was smooth underneath my touch.

I'd hugged her, held her, but this was a mistake.

Because I only wanted to explore her.

She nudged her tongue between my lips and whimpered when mine dueled with hers. Something in me came to life I hadn't known was dead. She'd intrigued me from the moment we met, but now that I'd tasted her?

I'm in trouble.

And I kissed her harder. Deeper. Longer.

Sadie's barks were the background to the most intimate moment of my life. And it was a chaotic perfection.

CHAPTER THIRTY-SIX

PEPPER

ARE WE KISSING?

Of course you are, crazy.

Why are you even thinking this?

Why are you thinking at all?

Just kiss him.

I couldn't close my eyes. I needed to see this. Be sure it was real.

Wow.

His mouth on mine felt . . . I couldn't describe it.

His hair in my fingers felt . . . like it was meant to be there.

His hands on my face felt . . . like I never wanted him to move them.

This wasn't like the last sloppy college kiss I'd had. It had something behind it I didn't understand. The feeling was foreign, yet not unpleasant.

Who was I? Some stuffy prude? *Unpleasant?*

It was spectacular—stars and moon aligning and all the fireworks stuff of fairy tales. And I didn't believe in fairy tales.

I could barely breathe.

My mind whirled.

And I felt everything.

This was the kiss of a man who knew exactly what he wanted. And if I'd been unclear before about what I desired, it had become abundantly clear.

I wanted him.

My knees went weak at the realization. I pulled back but was still fully in his grasp.

"Is that normal?" My voice was hoarse, as dazed sounding as I felt.

"Don't think so," he said, a little in awe.

Sadie's voice, on the other hand, was not hoarse. She continued to bark her demands in rapid succession.

Oh my word.

I'd just had the best kiss of my life, probably of anyone's life, to the sound of barking dogs. At least they couldn't tell Miss Adeline.

"I'd better . . ." I motioned in her direction.

Teague didn't immediately drop his hand. "We're doing that again."

"If you like the barking as mood music, I'd suggest six in the morning or six at night." *Pepper.* Was I flirting? Again?

"I'll keep that in mind." He smirked. "Um, Pepper? You've still got a hand in my hair."

"Oh." I dropped it like I realized I'd had my fingers on a burning stove.

"Mind if she tags along upstairs?" He scruffed Ash's head.

"Nope." I gripped the straps of my overalls and rocked back on my heels.

Why did I feel so awkward now? And why had he kissed me when I had morning breath . . .

I stared after him when they took off.

Miss Adeline appeared in the empty doorway and whistled. "My stars." She fanned her face as she used a fake southern drawl.

"Hush." I looked anywhere but at her for something to do but couldn't remember what was going on before the kiss.

I tossed Sadie a treat, which she happily smacked.

"Did you think I'd mind if you wanted to have a sleepover?" The woman could not be deterred. "You didn't have to sleep down here."

"It wasn't planned," I snipped before I let out a long sigh. "We have a big day ahead."

She squeezed my shoulders. "It'll all be fine. Always is."

I wished I had an ounce of her optimism. The glow of the kiss was gone, replaced by worry for the animals we were responsible for.

"And I mean that on all fronts," she said before I could respond.

"I don't want to talk about him." My exasperation seeped through my words.

"You're the one who just brought him up."

She won. Every. Single. Time.

The bell above the front door jingled. I tensed.

"We really need to keep that locked," I muttered. Unexpected visitors were not on my list of favorites at the moment. Except the Elliotts and Jacobses.

And Teague.

"Heyyy! Anybody home?"

I relaxed as another acceptable unexpected visitor appeared.

"Hey, Beau." I waved her into the back room. "What brings you by?"

"I just realized what I'm about to ask may get him in trouble." She shrugged. "You wouldn't happen to have seen my brother? He didn't come back to Lincoln's place last night. Annnd now if you don't know, I've just helped him screw things up with you."

She smacked herself in the forehead.

"Is he staying at your brother's?" Miss Adeline asked innocently. She knew how to make someone squirm and get info at once.

"Yeah. Just while—actually I don't know how long. But he has his own place," she said quickly. "This was a bad idea, wasn't it?"

"He's—"

"Where does he live?" Miss Adeline cut me off like a champ before I could put Beau out of her misery.

She shifted on her feet. "Well, I . . . he just moved and I haven't been by yet." Her words poured out in a rush.

Miss Adeline lifted a brow.

"But I think it's close by here." Beau didn't seem the type to easily cave.

But her odd behavior, not that I had more than a few hours of being around her to compare it to, raised my suspicions.

Why was she being so weird about Teague?

"I don't think he's ever mentioned it." Miss Adeline knew damn well he hadn't.

"He's pretty private." Beau hefted her purse on her shoulder. "Sorry to have bothered you." She looked at me. "Don't hold it against him. He probably stayed at the fire station. I honestly can't remember the last time he mentioned a girl."

"What's going on?" I asked.

She sagged against the wall. "I'm just worried about him. A lot's happened lately and when he wasn't up for breakfast and didn't answer his phone, my mind automatically went into overdrive."

Teague was lucky to have people around him who cared. He had family and friends and brothers at the fire station. Did he realize how fortunate he was?

Beau straightened. "I should've called you instead of barging in, but when he wasn't next door, I got really worried. I'll get out of your hair." She started for the exit.

"Next door?" My question stopped her.

I tried to think of what was on either side of us. The shop on one side had closed not that long ago. And on the other—

She appeared like she'd said too much and wished she could zip her lip. Instead she pointed to her left.

"His loft is right there."

CHAPTER THIRTY-SEVEN

TEAGUE

"BEAU?"

I hesitated at the top of the stairs when I found my sister at the bottom of them.

"You're fine. I'm going to go." She motioned toward the front door with her thumb.

"Why wouldn't I be fine?"

"No reason. I better jet."

I scowled. My sister was talking too fast.

"Beau." I exaggerated her name in warning.

"I was worried. You know how I get when I worry. So you can't be mad." She finger-waved and dashed for the door.

I plowed down the stairs after her but skidded to a stop at the look on Pepper's face.

"Beau," I called as she pushed out the exit.

"I'll see you in a little while." Her long coat flared behind her as she hurried away down the sidewalk.

When I turned around, Miss Adeline discreetly backed farther into the back room. Pepper looked like she'd been slapped and the initial surprise was wearing off.

"You live next door?" Each syllable was spoken slowly as if she wanted to get them right.

Crap. Beau and her big mouth. It wasn't like I cared if Pepper knew. Eventually I was going to have to tell her. But it got out of control and now I looked like a creep.

"I, uh—" I scratched the back of my neck. "I'd just moved in right before I met you." I sounded like my sister and her fast talking. "And then Beau came into town and I've been staying with my brother too and . . ."

She crossed her arms over her chest, clearly not impressed with my explanation. Or lack thereof.

"I just never got around to telling you." And I didn't want to look like a stalker. Except all those excuses sounded lame.

"Guess it makes more sense how you came up with groceries so quickly the first time you cooked for us," she said, but she was like stone. Unreadable.

"Yeah." I plowed my hand through my hair. "I wasn't exactly not telling you. I . . ." Damn it. I was so mixed up I didn't know what I was doing anymore.

"You don't owe me an explanation."

I froze. "I don't?"

"No."

"But you seem mad." I dropped my arm to my side.

She didn't say anything for a long time. When it came to Pepper, I couldn't seem to make the right moves. That kiss was definitely the right move. And I hoped to fall asleep with her again, even if my back wasn't too thrilled with me. But all the good things seemed to get erased by the stupid ones.

"It's like you're hiding something." She threw her hands up and paced. "But then you'll be so open. So I don't know if it's intentional or just happens that way. And what right do I really have anyway?"

Her words came out in a long, fast string. Almost as if she were talking to herself instead of me.

"You do things that make me trust you." She stopped in front of me. "And then you do things that make me doubt you."

"That's not my intention." Which was the pure absolute truth.

"It's a lot. Fast." She stepped closer. "We didn't exactly hit it off."

"If I'd have told you we were neighbors that first day, Muffy might've left me a present on my doorstep." I hoped we were moving past this. I hated conflict. Especially with her.

"Now that we know where you live, he might just yet."

The tension from before was gone from the set of her shoulders. Could she get over things this quickly?

"Muffy and I are pals now. He wouldn't do that." I snuck a hand to her hip.

"I wouldn't be so sure."

"I see how it is." I eased her closer. Strange how being near her soothed my stress and made my heart beat faster at the same time. "I'm sorry."

She placed her palm on my chest. "Beau caught me off guard. It made me question if you're hiding something."

"For a while, things between us were on thin ice. I wasn't sure how you'd take it if I was your creepy neighbor. Then I never found a good time." In retrospect, it was stupid. How could I tell her I couldn't stay next door now because it was too tempting to be near her?

Apparently, it didn't matter if I was next door, at my brother's, or in California. I'd still find my way to her.

Shit. We were near the front windows where anyone could see.

"Breakfast is getting cold." I hoped that didn't sound as false-cheerful to her as it did to me.

Her brows dipped. "Better not let it go to waste."

Relief that if she saw through my apprehension she hadn't pressed me on it coursed through me.

"Woman!" she called. "Time for breakfast."

And then Sadie barked all over again at the B word.

CHAPTER THIRTY-EIGHT

PEPPER

"DID you know he lived next door?"

I flipped on my turn signal and slowed at the intersection.

Miss Adeline choked on her tea. "What? How would I have known?"

She'd been suspiciously quiet on the matter. And she'd left me to handle the news on my own with Teague. Normally, she'd insert herself.

"Just wondering."

The dogs were quiet in the back of the van. I still felt guilty about having to do this. I didn't want to shuffle them around or leave them in someone else's care.

What other choice was there?

Miss Adeline patted my knee. "They'll be fine."

"I know."

The closer we got to Daniel and Vivian's, the slower I drove.

"When you've kept something from people, why'd you do it?"

I gripped the steering wheel. This woman and her insightful questions.

"It was none of their business."

She snickered. "That's a good reason for sure."

"Or if I cared about them, I didn't want them to get hurt."

She sobered but might as well have shouted *ding ding ding*.

"Why would it hurt me to know where he lived?" I asked, though I wasn't sure I was connecting the right dots. Because that would mean Teague cared about me.

"I don't know. But that boy's instinct is to protect, so you'll have to have a little faith in him." She casually sipped her tea as if dropping truth bombs were no big deal.

"He's been here. Even when he said he couldn't be."

Maybe I hadn't been around enough people in my adult life. Miss Adeline might be crafty, but she always said what she meant.

I had more trouble expressing my opinions, to people I didn't know that well, at least. So I understood not everyone was forthcoming.

But my feelings for Teague were all tangled up and they undermined my ability to read him.

"Honey, it doesn't hurt to have a friend."

Is that what he was? A friend?

She winked, and I groaned. She meant *that* kind of "friend."

"I've never spent the night with anyone," I blurted.

"You looked peaceful. More so than normal when you sleep with the dogs."

I nearly hit a parked car. "You're spying on me?"

She grabbed the door to steady herself. "Checking. Not spying." She pulled on her seatbelt as if to be sure it was secure. "Are you ever going to tell him why you like sleeping with them?"

Dang it. Was she trying to make me wreck?

"I'm not sure that's any of his business."

She made a hmph noise. "When it is, think about how you'd feel if he kept that from you."

"WELL. THEY SEEM OKAY."

Vivian worried her hands as we looked at the pile of dogs asleep in her living room. They seemed better than okay. Better than I was.

"All the excitement wore them out."

We'd walked them in the park across the street. They'd played with the mountain of toys the Elliotts and Jacobses had bought them. Then they crashed.

"We should head back," Miss Adeline said. "Actually, you should. I'm staying here."

"Pick out a room." Vivian gestured down the hall.

"I already have." Miss Adeline hooked an arm through mine.

"You have the food, right? We'll be back at six to walk them." Is this what mothers leaving their child in someone else's care for the first time felt like?

"We can handle it. But come by whenever you like." Vivian quirked her mouth to the side. "On second thought. Maybe a five-minute heads-up. Just so you don't walk in on something interesting." She widened her eyes like she had a juicy secret.

My face flamed. "Um, I'll definitely give you that warning."

Miss Adeline swatted me. "No fun. Either of you. I'm not calling before I come over."

"Suit yourself." Vivian shrugged.

"You've got my number?"

"In my phone." Vivian held up the device. "Written in the kitchen. The bedroom. And Daniel's study."

"Let me write it down for the foyer too." I dug in my pocket for a piece of paper.

Miss Adeline dragged me toward the door. "Thank you. We'll talk to you later."

When we were in the lobby, she elbowed me. "Worrywart much?"

"We've never done this before," I said defensively.

"Do you think I'd let this happen if I didn't fully believe it was the right thing to do?" She marched into the elevator while I remained rooted in place.

"No. No, I don't think you would." Why hadn't I considered that? Miss Adeline was every bit as invested in the dogs as I was.

The doors began to close and she stuck out her arm to stop them. "I knew you wanted to move in there too."

. . .

"THOUGHT Y'ALL would be gone longer than this."

Stone Jacobs sat with his feet propped on the desk and hands behind his head.

"We would've been if it were up to this one." Miss Adeline set her travel mug on the wood surface.

"We've already been through it a thousand times," I groaned. Then I flashed Stone a weary smile. "Looks like you survived dog sitting."

He was surrounded by zonked-out puppies.

"All good."

"Thanks for staying with them."

Stone had volunteered to help us load the dogs headed to their place. I hadn't felt comfortable leaving everyone else behind on their own, given the events of the last few days.

"Anytime." He dropped his feet to the floor. Three dogs popped up their heads. He patted one of them. "Just so you're aware, some dude in a suit came by. I didn't like the looks of him, so I didn't let him in."

"A suit?" Like the inspector? No. No. No. We had forty-eight hours to comply.

"Yeah. Not that I have a thing against guys in suits. Daniel is my best friend and he sleeps in one." Stone stood. "That guy banged on the door for a while, but once he figured out I wasn't opening up, he moved along."

My heart thumped a thousand miles an hour. "Any idea what he wanted?"

"Nah. But he wanted to come in pretty bad." He pointed to the door. "I'd keep that locked."

"It wasn't the inspector, was it?" Miss Adeline's voice was hard.

"Don't think so, ma'am." He tipped his ball cap. "If you have any trouble, call us."

"Thank you again."

I walked him out and locked the door behind him, triple checking it was secure.

"What do you think that was all about?" Miss Adeline flopped into the seat Stone just vacated.

I rested on the edge of the desk. "Don't know. But I'm thinking we need some curtains for the front windows."

We'd always had the windows uncovered like a storefront. There'd never been any reason to cover them. Sure, there were the occasional break-ins in the neighborhood, but no one ever bothered us. Besides, it would be kind of hard not to get caught with so many dog alarms.

"I think you're right."

I frowned. "Are you any good with colors?" I glanced helplessly toward the windows. My attire mostly consisted of overalls, jeans, shirts, and sweatshirts. I wasn't exactly up to speed on what looked good.

The dogs didn't care if I matched or not.

"I decorated the apartment, didn't I?" Miss Adeline lifted her chin.

"You did. How could I forget?" I pushed off the desk. "Do you mind holding down the fort for a little while?"

"Are you gonna tell me where you're off to?"

I grabbed my coat. "Maybe when I get back."

CHAPTER THIRTY-NINE

TEAGUE

"YOU'RE quiet because of where we're headed. Not because you're mad at me, right?"

Beau shifted in her seat.

"I'm not mad at you." I focused on the street ahead. We weren't far from the cemetery. I shouldn't have driven. I wasn't in the right frame of mind.

"I didn't mean to blurt out your business." She fiddled with the fabric of her black dress.

"I know you didn't."

"Are you okay?"

I felt her stare but didn't look over at her. "Not really."

"Is she talking to you?"

I willed myself to have patience. "Yes. Everything is fine with Pepper."

She pointed to the curb. "There's a spot."

I parallel parked the truck but didn't immediately turn it off. I'd made it through the church service, but I hadn't heard a word of it. Though Cassano had been in a casket at the front, it still didn't seem true.

Watching someone lowered into the ground . . . that was when it would get real.

Beau touched my arm. "You can do this."

Ellen was counting on me to carry Cassano to his grave. It was the least I could do for her. But if it weren't for me, would we even be here?

I turned off the engine and shoved out of the truck. Beau had her door open by the time I came around to help her out.

She hooked her arm in mine as we trudged toward the cemetery. With every step, the past and present mingled. It was the same as that day all those years ago. Gloomy. Heavy.

The cemetery was different, but it might as well be the same. I was five and thirty-nine at the same time. There was no distinction between my mother's funeral and Cassano's.

I'd held Beau's hand back then. She was so little and hadn't said a word during our mother's services despite usually being a chatterbox.

Lincoln had held mine.

But he wasn't here today because I hadn't asked him to be.

Beau dug her fingers into my arm.

"Wanna ease up a bit?"

Her gaze was glued to the person waiting for us on the sidewalk just ahead. If anything, her grip tightened.

"Cal." I thrust out my hand.

He grabbed it and shook. "Teague. Long time, man."

We'd been in the same class in the fire academy and started out at the same station. Shortly after, he'd been moved and we only saw each other occasionally.

"Too long."

His eyes drifted to my sister, who stood stiffly, still latched onto me.

"Beau." He flicked his chin at her.

"Hello, Cal." The greeting was acid. She might as well have said, "Piss off."

His nostrils flared but we fell in stride toward the cemetery. "Sorry about Cassano. Way I heard it, he wouldn't have made it at all without you."

"He *didn't* make it." That was why we were at his funeral. Whether I got him out from under that bed or he died in a hospital, the result was the same. Maybe this way was worse. For a short time his family had hope.

I'd had hope.

Cal nodded. "You did all you could."

I clamped my lips together. I didn't want to talk about this. And after the service Ellen had invited—no, insisted—that I come over to their house for the family gathering. There would be more of the same. Outward pats on the back, while inwardly they all blamed me. As they should.

The bite of pain from Beau's vice grip on my arm finally registered. "Will you loosen up?"

She glared, but I didn't miss the flash of hurt on her face. Damn it. I hadn't meant to snap.

She dropped her arm altogether.

"If you need someone to hold onto, you can hang on to me." Cal offered his arm.

"I'd rather hold on to a live wire." She straightened her shoulders and stared straight ahead.

"It's the same thing, sweetheart."

Whatever feud they appeared to have was none of my concern. Not today.

The hearse loomed in front of us. I felt nothing. Like I was a shell of a man, somehow walking to a place I didn't want to be.

I had to go on autopilot. Had to shut out the threatening emotion. This was Cassano's day. One to honor him.

Thinking about anything other than that was selfish.

A low rumble of somber greetings came from the group of men surrounding the back of the hearse. There were a few shoulder slaps and hugs, then everyone resumed looking at their feet.

"Keep my sister company?" I may have just started another world war with that request, but I didn't want Beau to be alone. She knew a lot of people here from hanging around when she was younger, though it had been years since she'd seen most of them.

Judging from the incinerating death glare from her direction before she stalked toward the gravesite, I'd guess she wasn't too happy with me. Cal was on her heels, obviously loyal to me, no matter what my sister wanted.

The funeral director swung open the back door of the hearse. Even though I'd already seen the coffin today, I still lost my breath.

I planted my feet to steady myself and braced for the moment the polished wood would hit my hands.

Seconds seemed like years as we marched forward toward the hollowed earth.

We eased the coffin to the stand. Ellen kissed each of our cheeks. I bristled at the simple affection I didn't deserve.

I found my place next to Beau. I couldn't go through this service without my family close by.

As the priest opened his Bible, a hand clamped on my shoulder.

Lincoln.

I nodded in gratitude of his support. He squeezed and flanked my side.

There were two people in the world I could count on no matter what. Some people didn't even have one.

The words of the priest were a low buzz of background noise. As I stared at the coffin, all I could see was the fire.

"GO. *If you don't get out of here, we'll both die."*

"I'm not letting you be a marshmallow."

I'D KEPT that promise but failed him anyway. My throat closed as if I were back in the smoke. I held in the cough I wanted to let out. It was like I was in that house without my oxygen tank.

Spots dotted my vision. An arm linked through mine again but it wasn't enough to help me breathe.

Just a few more minutes. A few more minutes.

I could make it through this. If I could get out of my own head, I'd have a better chance. But the rain started to fall and suddenly my perspective was eye level to the coffin. A white one with deep pink roses on top.

Mom.

An umbrella opened above my head. People stirred around us.

"Teague." Beau's soft voice dragged me back to reality. "It's over."

But I couldn't move. I wanted to run. But I was stuck.

The crowd dispersed. In the distance, a welcomed sight in a rain-coat and overalls leaned against the tree. And I could finally breathe air into my lungs.

I took a full breath.

She silently acknowledged me but remained in place.

Pepper.

Maybe I had three people I could count on no matter what.

"Ready to go?" Lincoln's worried stare awaited me.

"Yeah."

When I looked back for Pepper, she was gone.

CHAPTER FORTY

PEPPER

"CURTAINS INSTALLED TOMORROW."

I shrugged off my raincoat and hung it on the coatrack. Water dripped onto the floor.

I shook out my wet hair. "That's great news. I'm not going to ask how you managed that so quickly."

Miss Adeline pretended to buff her nails. "Magic."

I surveyed the room. Muffy trotted over, and I bent to pet him. "It feels different in here."

We'd had such a crazy busy day, I hadn't stopped to notice . . . well, anything. The dogs from the New Jersey track hadn't been with us long, but there was an emptiness without them here.

"Vivian called. Said everyone is fine."

I appreciated her thoughtfulness to check in. Though we'd only dropped off the dogs a few hours ago, I was still apprehensive. Had we dumped too much responsibility on them?

"That's good." I shivered, the cold setting into my bones. "No visitors?"

That inspector might be back at any time. But I was thinking of closing the door separating the front and back area and hiding away out of sight until the curtains were up. Maybe that was the coward's way, but I really didn't want to see that man again.

"All quiet." She leaned back in her chair and studied me. "You going to tell me where you went off to in such a hurry?"

I slid to the floor. Muffy crawled into my lap and Ash edged closer so she was against my leg.

"To the funeral of the fireman who was hurt in the fire where Teague found Ash." I rubbed Muffy's belly. "I mean, I didn't go to the service. Just to the graveside. To check on him." The words tumbled out in a torrent. "Is that weird?"

"No," Miss Adeline said carefully. "What made you decide to do that?"

"Teague seemed pretty shaken up about it. I wanted to be there for him." My answer was automatic and quick. I hadn't thought much about what I was doing at the time. I simply acted on instinct. And it had been easy enough to find the place and time of the services from the write-up in the newspaper.

Although I hadn't necessarily meant for him to see me, I was glad he had. So he'd know I supported him.

Bark. Bark. Bark.

I checked the clock on the wall. "Already that time, Sadie?" How was it already time for their supper? "I just sat down," I complained as I patted her on the head.

She ducked and kept right on barking.

Ash joined in for a couple of barks.

We looked at her in surprise.

"Not you too?" I tickled her foot.

"That one is teaching them bad habits." Miss Adeline shook her finger at Sadie before she stood.

I eased Muffy off my lap and got to my feet. That dog had us all trained.

MY PHONE CHIMED WITH A TEXT.

A video appeared on the screen from Vivian. When she'd said they had lots of help, she must've meant it. There were five men walking our dogs down the sidewalk. Two of them I recognized as Daniel and Stone.

Miss Adeline looked over my shoulder and whistled. "If that wouldn't convince people to adopt a dog, I don't know what would."

She was right. The men were beyond good looking. "What about some of your calendar boys?"

She tapped me on the head. "You're a genius."

Another text came in. This time it was a video of five women walking dogs. Again, I knew Vivian and Muriella but not the others.

"That one would work too."

A second later my phone rang and I swiped to answer.

"See? Told you we have it handled." Vivian's breathless voice sounded in my ear.

"We definitely see." I pushed my spoon around in my empty bowl. "Thanks for sending the videos."

It was a relief to know they seemed to be getting on okay. And I was glad they had help . . . a lot of it. Even though Miss Adeline and I were pros at taking care of a large number of dogs, it was hard. For people who weren't used to it, it could be overwhelming.

Looked like I'd been worried for no reason.

"Thought you'd like that. I sent the one of the boys for Miss Adeline."

I snorted. "She approved."

"Oh I definitely approve," she chimed in.

"Everyone is fed, walked, and either sleeping or playing with toys." One squeaked to emphasize her point.

"No trouble?"

"None. They're all sweet and well-behaved." There was a pause. "Well, one rascal found our bed and has decided it's his."

I winced. "They're instinctive about the space they want."

"He's on Daniel's side. Looks like my husband will need to find somewhere else to sleep."

A growl rumbled through the phone and Vivian squeaked. "Fine.

We'll make room for you." Her voice sounded as if she'd turned away from the phone.

"I'll come walk them before bed." It was almost time to get started on that.

"No. No. We've got it handled. By the time you get over here, we'll have it done."

I tried to gauge if she meant that. If things were really going as well as she made out or if she was trying to placate me.

"I don't—"

"Everyone is fine. Come by tomorrow if you want. Take a load off tonight."

I drummed my fingers on the kitchen table. A bone-deep weariness set in. "If you're sure . . ."

"I'm sure. Now stop worrying."

We ended the call, and I dropped my phone on the table. Lightning lit up the sky and a roll of thunder cracked behind it.

"This is going to be fun."

"I checked a while ago. Looks like the weather's set in for the night." Miss Adeline picked up my bowl and put it in the sink.

"You're going to have to be quick." I scratched behind Ash's ears. She wagged her tail. "You ready?" That tail went faster. "Let me get my raincoat."

THE ALLEY behind the building didn't have the safest vibe, but somehow the front seemed more dangerous. Exposed.

"C'mon, you two."

Muffy and Sadie were having no part of doing their business fast. The frigid rain was coming down in sheets, yet they piddled down the alley like it was a perfect summer day.

Sadie looked back at me, illuminated by one of the lights on the building.

"We are *not* going all the way to the park."

I swore her expression was *wanna bet?* Not particularly. She'd win. Just like always.

She strolled forward, and Muffy seemed content to trot beside her. We reached the street, she looked both ways, then did her business.

Muffy sniffed and did the same.

"Thank you," I said as I picked up the mess in a plastic bag. "Let's get back inside."

They moseyed back no matter how I coaxed. Rain pelted us, the surrounding buildings doing nothing to shield us from the fat drops.

I tossed the waste in the dumpster and dug in my pocket for the keys. Sadie stamped her feet by the door.

"Oh now you're impatient to get in?"

Bark.

"I'm hurrying," I said as I fumbled through the keys.

Woof. Woof.

I paused, on full alert now that Muffy had joined in. When I lifted my head, a shadowy figure slid by the van.

Sadie's and Muffy's barks grew more ferocious. Dang it. I didn't have any Mace. Of all the times to be careless. I'd locked the back door to be safe but hadn't considered outside threats.

I found the key, shoved it in the lock, shaking as I turned it.

The dogs' barks turned to tugs. They jumped and wagged their tails at the person now drenched in light.

Teague.

CHAPTER FORTY-ONE

TEAGUE

I DIDN'T ASK to come inside.

I just did.

And the second the door shut behind me, I backed her against it and slammed my mouth onto hers.

She whimpered, dropped the leashes, and fisted my coat.

I wasn't gentle like she deserved.

But my need to express my gratitude was urgent.

Again, she hadn't said a word to me at the funeral, but her presence had been enough. She'd seen me through another tragic day.

The dogs jumped as if they wanted to join in. I snapped my fingers and they sat.

Pepper yanked me closer and kissed me back like she'd been waiting her whole life to do it.

There was a wildness about her.

She drew me in with her spirit.

And her heart.

Our mouths moved together, conveying what words never could. She never closed her eyes when we kissed. Like she wanted to *see* me. I loved that.

I pushed the hood of her rain jacket off her head. Her hair and face were wet. She wore no makeup. Pepper didn't need it.

She was beautiful in the purest sense.

We grew more frantic; if we didn't convey our message right that instant it would be lost for good. I pressed her farther into the door. Our bodies were molded together, yet it still wasn't close enough.

Need pulsed through my veins with a vengeance I'd never felt.

She shivered.

Instinct kicked in.

She was soaking wet. And cold.

I ripped my mouth off hers.

"You'll catch. A cold." I spoke between harsh breaths.

"I don't care." She stretched her neck toward me and brushed her lips across mine.

I groaned.

"But I do."

She screwed up her face, and I was secretly pleased she wanted me too.

I took her hand and led her toward the stairs. The dogs raced ahead of us. Sadie was slower as she hopped up the steps, but we let her set the pace to the top.

"Look what the cat dragged in." Miss Adeline set her book down and smirked. "My mistake. We don't have any cats."

Pepper snickered.

Miss Adeline's razor-sharp eyes zeroed in on where my fingers were twined with Pepper's. "You ready to take a stand?"

I swallowed hard. The alarm bells and instinct I had to stay away from Pepper to protect her from my father had been overridden by the ones that kept me coming back. A war raged inside of me.

Pepper was winning.

Is that why I was here? To take a stand?

"I . . ." I didn't know. Only that I kept ending up here. With her.

"You don't have to answer that." Pepper sent Miss Adeline a pointed look. "She's full of nosy questions."

"Looks like my next one should be where's the mop?"

My coat was drenched, as well as my hair and the bottom of my pants. Pepper wasn't much better.

"Let me take your coat." Pepper slipped her fingers under the collar and gently pried it off.

She opened a closet door and hooked it over the top before she shrugged hers off and hung it on the doorknob.

"Have you eaten?" Miss Adeline pushed out of her chair before I could answer. "We had chicken tortilla soup. And before you get all excited, no we didn't make it. That's what the deli down the street is for."

There'd been enough food for a buffet at the get together at Cassano's house. I hadn't touched any of it. I couldn't.

"I haven't."

"I'd suggest you go home and change clothes, but what's the point?" She pulled a bowl out of the cabinet.

"Miss Adeline!" Pepper might as well have clutched her proverbial pearls.

"What? He'd just get them all wet too." She turned on the stove where a pot was already sitting. "Did you think I meant because he's going to take them off soon?"

Pepper closed her eyes and I half wondered if she was going to run into the closet to hide.

"I honestly have no idea why you'd subject yourself to this," she finally muttered.

"Go take a shower before you catch a cold," Miss Adeline said. "You've been out in that weather too long."

"Can you handle being alone with her?" Pepper asked.

I'd rather be alone with Pepper. In the shower. But this wasn't the time.

"I think I've got it."

Miss Adeline didn't speak again until the sound of the water turned on down the hall.

"Sit." For a second, I didn't know if she was talking to me or one of the dogs, but they were all already stretched out around the floor. "She might let you avoid my questions, but I won't."

She stirred the warming soup with her back to me.

I obeyed and took one of the chairs at the kitchen table.

"I realize you haven't courted my girl. But I see the way you look at her. And you clearly can't stay away." She turned and lasered into me with shrewd eyes. "So when the time comes to fight, what are you gonna do?"

I folded my hands on the table and looked down. The answer was no clearer than it had been when she asked a few minutes ago. It wasn't simple.

I'd already broken promises to myself and to Pepper by recklessly continuing to defy my father. It was dangerous to be here. Pepper and Miss Adeline had already had to split up their family.

Part of me questioned if somewhere deep down I believed they were better off if I were here to help protect them instead of leaving them on their own. Yes, it put them on my father's radar. But they were already there.

I didn't know what kind of perverse pleasure he took from destroying innocent people's lives. And I shouldn't matter to him. I didn't matter to him.

She ladled some soup in a bowl and set it in front of me. "I've never backed away from hard times. You bring a fresh kind of trouble with you." She sank down in the adjacent chair. "But I won't go through hell for a coward."

I froze mid-lift of the spoon.

I'm not a coward.

Then I thought about the way I'd jetted out of here the day my father arrived. How I'd jumped when he'd summoned me.

But I did it for her.

If Pepper weren't in the picture, my father could've set fire to my shoes and I still wouldn't have set foot in his office.

Did being motivated by fear make me a coward?

"Believe" by Cher blared from my pocket. I nearly dropped the spoon but managed to hang onto it and dig my phone out.

"Yo. Five alarm on West Fourteenth and Tenth. Need all hands.

Can you make it?" The alarm screamed in the background along with shouts.

"I'm not far. Bring my gear." I threw down the spoon, shoved out of my chair, and pocketed my phone in one swift motion. "Massive fire. I gotta go."

I grabbed my coat and raced down the stairs. My mind was in overdrive, mapping the intersection in my head. The back door of Grey Paws slammed behind me.

I sprinted down the alley. We were on West Seventeenth and Eighth Avenue. West Fourteenth was a few blocks away.

Rain pelted my face as I ran. In two blocks, the red strobe lights of a fire truck beamed through the night sky. Off in the distance, another siren wailed.

A car skidded to a stop, narrowly missing me in the crosswalk. The horn blew, but I ignored it.

Flames shot through the darkness. And when the blaze came into view, I realized I'd been here only a few days ago.

Pepper's park.

CHAPTER FORTY-TWO

PEPPER

"YOU RAN HIM OFF."

I towel-dried my hair as I walked into the kitchen—minus a certain someone.

"For your information, he had an emergency call."

I frowned. "Everything okay?"

My mind jumped to worst-case scenarios. Had something happened to his brother or sister? Someone else at work?

"Big fire. Sounds like it's close by."

That sinking feeling intensified. He was headed straight for danger. I admired his bravery but hated the threat.

Miss Adeline rinsed out the bowl and set it in the sink. "Want some tea to warm you up?"

"No. I actually think I might dry my hair and go to bed."

Sadie perked up at yet another of her favorite B words.

"Pepper."

I stopped fiddling with the towel. "Yeah."

She stared at me a minute. "Sometimes we have to figure out how we feel before we're ready to."

"I don't know what that means." I wandered over to stand next to her.

"You will one day." She took my cheeks in her frail hands. "I love you and I'm with you all the way."

"I love you too."

The old woman I adored wandered away with several dogs behind her and more of her mysterious wisdom. It had been a while since she'd bestowed any of those nuggets. Miss Adeline had always been amazingly good at walking the line between telling me about life and letting me figure it out for myself.

Huh.

For as much as she liked to talk, she never tried to dictate how I lived. That was another reason I admired her. Even if she did meddle at times.

While I didn't quite get what she was telling me now, I had a pretty good idea it had to do with Teague.

How did I feel about him?

I propped my hip on the counter. Sadie put her head back down and sighed.

Did I really need to know now? We were . . . doing whatever it was we were doing. It seemed almost minute to minute.

Which wasn't that much different than how everything in my life had been up to this point. Except Miss Adeline. And the dogs.

They were the constants who kept me grounded.

Before that, what I believed was steady and sure washed out from under me before I realized what was happening. I never planned to end up living in the dog kennels at a racetrack in Virginia.

At the time, it seemed hopeless.

Turned out that was the best thing to ever happen to me.

But the last person I'd truly let in was Miss Adeline. I'd allowed Teague into the first walls, but there were many more surrounding my heart.

He seemed capable of battling his way through every locked gate inside me. Did I want him there?

By the rapid pace we were moving, it seemed I did.

I liked his heart.

I liked his determination.

I liked his spirit.

I really liked his kisses.

What did that mean though? This was all new to me. I hadn't experienced any of these things in my mature life.

You ready to take a stand?

I didn't know what Miss Adeline's question for Teague meant either. The way he'd stiffened, I had to believe he did.

"If she'd offered bourbon, I might've taken her up on it."

Sadie ignored me.

I squeezed the towel around my hair again. "C'mon. You can bark at the hair dryer."

She shot to her feet. The pitter-patter of paws on the hardwood floor erased some of the stress of the day. It was my favorite sound.

Muffy flopped on my bed while Sadie cruised past to the bathroom. Ash and Lucky stood at the foot of the bed, unsure who to follow.

The second I turned on the hair dryer, the barking commenced. I was lost in the hum. Thoughts of that scorching kiss besieged me.

Teague had a way of sneaking up on me whether he was present or not.

I wanted another kiss. The urgency and frenzy of it.

The certainty of his touch. He was never tentative.

And I needed him to be sure.

Something deep burned within me. It was like a tiny flame had escalated into a ball of fire. A desire so hot it threatened to consume me.

I switched off the dryer and shed my sweatshirt. When I saw my reflection in the mirror, I looked the same, but the inside pieces of me were shifting.

I traded my flannel pajama pants for an old pair of sleep shorts and crawled into bed. Sadie jumped up and lay on my pillow before I could put my head on it. I grabbed another pillow and scooted her over to make a little room. Ash snuggled next to Sadie. Lucky settled on the floor.

Exhaustion set in, but my mind worked too fast. Was Teague okay? Had they contained the fire?

I checked my phone. It was barely after nine.

I rolled over. Sadie's face was right in mine. She sniffed and licked my nose.

"You're crazy." I rubbed her cheeks and kissed her head.

In the light through the window, Muffy gave the two of us a *go to sleep* look. These dogs constantly kept me in check.

Maybe I'd never needed a man in my life or my bed because I had them.

"You like him." I patted Ash's side. She was doing well. Almost thriving considering what she'd been through.

Her tail thumped as if she knew I was talking about Teague.

"What would've happened if he hadn't been called away?"

She looked at me with those luminous eyes.

"I don't know either."

Bzzz. Bzzz.

My stomach dropped at the text alert. Were the dogs at the Elliots' okay? Gah, I was such a worrier.

My stomach dropped again for a different reason when I read the message.

Meet me at the back door.

CHAPTER FORTY-THREE

TEAGUE

WHERE ARE HER CLOTHES?

A gaggle of dogs greeted me as I slipped through the open door.

"Heyyy." I gave each of them some attention but not because I was a saint who loved dogs. I *did* love dogs.

But if I didn't do something to distract myself from that camisole and those short shorts, I'd be in trouble.

She folded her arms and rubbed them.

Mission failed.

All I saw was smooth skin just begging for me to explore.

"You cold?" I straightened, focusing on her face.

Her hair is down.

I couldn't remember ever seeing her without a bun or lopsided ponytail or braids. Her dark locks looked temptingly soft.

The woman was going to completely unravel me.

Except I didn't think she was trying at all.

"I'm fine." Goose bumps rose on her bare legs. Down my gaze went. Her overalls usually hid the shape. I had no idea how slender and toned they'd be. "Everything okay? Miss Adeline said there was a big fire."

All at once, it felt like I was back outside in the cold rain.

"Yeah." That wasn't a lie, but it wasn't the truth either. The fire was contained, but everything most definitely wasn't okay.

"You changed."

She ran her eyes down my body, taking in my sweater and jeans, and heat simmered in them.

"I grabbed a shower after and . . ." *Wanted to see you.* But I couldn't say that. "Did I wake you?"

"No," she said sleepily. "Want to come up?"

She held out her hand.

More than anything. After I left the fire, all I could think of was getting back to her.

I stared at it a moment before twining my fingers with her warm ones.

The dogs led us up the stairs and straight to her bedroom. Most of them pounced on the bed and claimed their space.

If the plan was for all of us to fit in that queen-sized bed, I didn't think it was going to work.

"I don't have any pajamas your size." Pepper stood on the edge of the bed with the comforter fisted.

"Good thing I don't wear any."

She swallowed hard. "Oh."

Gently, she adjusted Sadie, who was already on a pillow. She slid under the covers and pulled them up to her chin.

I kicked off my boots, pulled my sweater over my head, and shoved my jeans to the floor. Pepper watched my every move like she'd never seen anyone undress.

The bed creaked when I sat on the edge. Ash inched toward my lap.

"Wanna let me in?"

She licked my hand in response.

"She's glad you're here," Pepper said quietly.

I twisted. "Are you?"

She nodded and I finagled my way under the covers. A wall of dogs separated us.

"This isn't going to work."

I climbed back out of bed, eased three dogs to the spot I'd just occupied, and rounded the foot.

"Scoot over," I said to Pepper when I reached her side.

We smushed together in our half of the bed. One of my ass cheeks and part of my leg was hanging off, but I didn't care.

I pulled her against me and kissed the side of her hair.

She snuggled into my chest, her body a perfect fit.

"You smell like fire."

I fingered her hair. It was as soft as it looked. "No matter how much I shower, that scent lingers."

"I like it . . . except I guess it represents destruction."

She was more right than she probably knew. I wanted to shield her from the unpleasant. Have this moment where we held each other and didn't have to think about anything beyond these walls.

But that wasn't how real life worked.

"The fire . . ." I fiddled with a strand of her hair. "It was the park."

Her brows dipped. "The park?"

"Down the block." I pulled her closer, needing to cocoon her as I broke the news. "The one we met in a few days ago. *Their* park."

A strangled noise escaped her. "Is it . . . bad?"

There was fear twinged with the heartbreak. Those dogs loved that park. It may have been small but that was their special place.

"It's gone."

She covered her mouth, and I eased her head to my chest. Her shoulders moved up and down, not with tears, but heavy breaths . . . like she couldn't catch hers.

We lay like that for I didn't know how long. She'd had a long day. A hard one, even if she hadn't said the words. And I'd just added to it. While I wished I could've kept the news from her, no way was I going to let her find out when she took the dogs tomorrow.

She lifted her head. Pain seeped from every line on her face. "How?"

I hesitated. She deserved more than my cowardice.

"Arson."

The blaze had shot high into the sky despite the rain and wind. We'd worked frantically to keep it from spreading to nearby buildings. Once it was under control, several melted barrels were in the center of the park.

"Who would burn such a special place?" There was an innocence in her tone, like she hadn't seen enough bad things to understand evil. I wanted to do everything in my power to keep her that way.

"Children play there." The innocence had turned to anger.

"None of them were hurt."

She pounded on my chest. "But they will be tomorrow when their favorite place is gone."

Pepper wasn't just talking about the kids in the neighborhood. She meant her children. The four-legged ones.

"It's not like lightning struck a tree and a terrible thing happened," she cried. "Someone destroyed the park on purpose. What kind of monster does that?"

I brushed my thumb across her cheek. This woman was brave. Had the kindest soul. And I wanted to hurt—badly—the person responsible for breaking her heart.

"The worst kind."

I didn't know how, but I was going to fix this for her. For them.

Ash moved so that she lay across our feet. Like she knew we both needed the comfort.

"Will you find out who did this?" Pepper asked through gritted teeth.

"The investigation unit will try."

A dissatisfied noise came from her direction. We were both well aware how many unsolved crimes there were in the city.

My phone trilled from my pants pocket.

I didn't move.

"You should get that." Pepper nudged me.

Reluctantly, I got out of bed and swiped the phone.

"Yo. You ain't gonna believe this." Burke practically screamed in my ear. "All them barrels?"

"Yeah?" I switched the phone to my other ear and got back in bed.

I slid an arm around Pepper's shoulders, who was looking at me with curiosity.

"Every one of them had a body in it."

CHAPTER FORTY-FOUR

PEPPER

SNIFF. *Sniff. Sniff.*

A nose in my ear stirred me. I was surprised I'd found any sleep at all. It had evaded me for hours.

The park.

Losing that space almost felt like losing a friend.

I hadn't realized how important it was to our family until it was gone.

Sniff. Sniff.

I pried my eyes open.

For the second day in a row, Teague's beautiful face was my welcome to the land of the living. This morning, there was no peace in his features. He was draped across me as if afraid I'd escape.

Muffy sniffed more urgently. I cupped his face in a silent *I'll take you out.*

Maneuvering so I didn't wake Teague? That was going to be an interesting feat.

The second I moved, his lids popped open.

"Sorry." I screwed my face up in apology. "Muffy's got to go out."

He blinked a few times as if trying to get his bearings. "I'll take him."

Like he understood, Muffy leaped off the bed and stood at Teague's side, wagging his tail.

He slid to his feet. In the light of day, I had a much better look at his chiseled torso. Bruises, now turning yellow, spread across his stomach.

"Does that hurt?" I pointed at his skin but didn't touch it.

He looked down as if attempting to figure out what I meant, then shrugged. "Don't think about it anymore."

Robotically, he tugged on his jeans and sweater. He was silent, closed off. But I wasn't sure if it was because he was tired or something else.

I hopped up. "I'll go with you."

I layered up, and after a peek out the window, I put on my heavy coat instead of my rain jacket.

Excited dogs trotted to the front door. The old pipes creaked through the walls. *Miss Adeline must be in the shower.*

I scribbled a quick note and left it propped against her favorite tea mug.

"I'll take three, you take two?" I offered Teague Ash's leash.

He grunted a response. Maybe he wasn't a morning person. But this was the opposite of the man I'd been with yesterday.

Once we burst out into the alley, the dogs pulled and yanked, anxious to go. Muffy stopped and lifted his leg on a patch of weeds growing next to the building.

Teague and Ash patiently waited but quickly caught up to us. Out of habit and routine, the dogs led us in the direction of the park.

"Don't do this."

His voice was rough, pleading.

"I need to see it."

The dogs didn't realize what lay ahead. And I hated for them to find out. Because they would know their favorite place was gone.

Selfishly, I had to see what was left. Just how bad it was.

I smelled the destruction before I saw it.

Smoldering ashes dotted what used to be the park. Everything was charred. The trees. The gate, which was a tangled heap.

Nothing but a metal leg remained of the bench I'd sat on with Teague what seemed like a lifetime ago.

I was rooted on the sidewalk across the street, unable to do anything but stare in horror. Muffy sat and cocked his head. Sadie pointed her nose to the air and sniffed. Ash was glued to Teague's side. She knew what that scent was all too well.

"How do you do this?" The wreckage was almost crippling.

"I don't know how someone could do this." His jaw was hard, knuckles white as he fisted the leashes.

"No. How do *you* do this? How can you stand to witness this every single day?"

My insides would be as charred as this park if I had to constantly live through that. Sure, this park affected me directly, but look at what fire had done to Ash. To Cassano. And how many others who'd lost everything.

I turned my head. It was too hard to take in.

"I couldn't save my mother."

He spoke so quietly I almost missed it. But his words twisted at my heart. Or maybe it was the unspoken ones.

He was trying to make up for that by helping other people.

The vulnerability in his expression nearly knocked me to my knees. Had he ever admitted that to anyone . . . or himself?

I opened my mouth to tell him she was proud but snapped it closed. I didn't know her. If she was anything like Teague, she would've been so honored at the man he was.

But those were words for someone else to tell him. Someone who had the right to.

"I'm sorry I couldn't save your park. I tried."

A burden no one should have to carry weighted him.

"No." I shifted the leashes so I could touch his shoulder. "You did everything you could."

I had zero doubt about that.

"We should head back." I pointed with my head in the direction of Grey Paws.

Silently, we strolled. At this early hour, there was little noise around us as the city came to life. Even Sadie behaved.

"Will they find out who those people are?"

I'd been horrified to learn what they'd discovered in the incendiary barrels. What motivated humans to hurt others, I'd never understand.

"Depends on if things break our way."

"I hope they get justice."

He nodded once. "Me too."

CHAPTER FORTY-FIVE

TEAGUE

THIS SHOULDN'T HAVE HAPPENED.

I couldn't get Pepper's horrified face out of my head when she took in the park. She'd been quiet ever since. Her shoulders hunched as we worked together to feed the dogs.

Where would she take them now?

Ash pawed at my leg. I kneeled beside her. "I gotta go to work soon."

She burrowed against me as I rubbed her ears.

"My shift's twenty-four on, so I won't be by tonight. Promise me you'll eat?"

She licked my face. I hoped that was a yes.

"Miss Adeline will be devastated." There was a hollowness to Pepper's sarcasm.

"You never did tell me exactly how you met."

She fidgeted with straightening the counter, even though everything was already in order.

"I called her about some abused dogs at a track," she said as if choosing her words carefully.

"I gathered that." Why wouldn't she look at me? "How'd you know about them? Did you work there?"

She knotted the towel used to dry the dog bowls in her fingers. I rose to my full height and knitted my brow.

"I lived there."

She dropped the towel and bent to pet Sadie like a default mechanism.

"Like a caretaker?" But that didn't make sense. If the dogs were under her care, she wouldn't have needed to contact Miss Adeline. She'd never abuse an animal . . . or anyone.

"Like a homeless person."

Pepper kept full eye contact as she spoke. I tried to control my reaction, but my brows shot up. *Homeless?*

This woman worked harder than anyone I'd ever met . . . including my brother. And that was saying a lot. I simply could not imagine the scenario she described.

Then the image of her sleeping so soundly with the dogs crashed into my brain.

Was that why she was so comfortable with them?

She spread her arm, motioning to the dogs surrounding us. "We're all rescues."

Underneath the acceptance of her situation was a hint of defensiveness.

"Pepper—"

"Please don't tell me you're sorry. It ended up being the best thing that ever happened to me. I'm here." She stroked Sadie more spastically.

"I—" I didn't know what to say. Other than it hurt and made me angry she'd ever had to experience that.

If she hadn't met Miss Adeline, where would she be?

She refused to look at me, and I stood there like an idiot who couldn't think of anything to say.

"I get it if you don't want—"

My phone chimed.

Don't want what?

But she didn't finish. Not in the two minutes it took for my phone to alert me again that I had an unread text message.

The air turned awkward, like we were strangers. Like we hadn't spent last night in each other's arms. Like those kisses hadn't happened. Like we hadn't shared anything we normally kept to ourselves.

I pulled out my phone.

My office. Half an hour.

"It's the captain. I have to go."

I didn't want to leave. Not like this when I wouldn't be able to see her until at least tomorrow.

"Who wants a treat?" She moved toward the container and carried it away from the back door. All the dogs obediently followed. Except Ash. Who stayed pressed to my leg.

I stroked her head. "I'll see you soon." Though I wasn't sure if that was true. "Go get a treat."

She stayed next to me.

The other dogs were in a semi-circle around Pepper, mostly patiently waiting for a dog biscuit.

"Pepper."

She tossed a treat to Sadie. "Thank you for everything." She wouldn't look at me. And I didn't fault her that. She'd told me something intimately personal and humiliating. I imagined it wasn't a fact she shared often, if ever.

I stalked toward her, careful not to step on any dogs. I leaned forward and kissed her cheek. "This changes nothing." I was not a coward.

I HOPPED out of my truck at the station.

Heavy.

That was how everything felt. These past few weeks had been a lot.

Normally, I'd be glad to have a long shift. This was where I was meant to be. My extended family.

Maybe the twenty-four on was a blessing. I could get out of my head for a bit and hopefully have some perspective.

But I hated how I'd left things with Pepper.

She could probably use a minute to sort things out for herself too, but I hated the way she'd withdrawn from me.

I *felt* it.

And I didn't like the distance.

Did she think I'd want nothing to do with her because of her past?

On the drive over, the farther away I got, the more it seemed that way. I didn't want her to believe that. Hadn't she seen by now, there was nothing that could keep me away?

Except she practically pushed me out the door.

"Yo." Burke fell in step beside me as we approached the firehouse.

"You back on? I thought you worked last night?"

"Got a message to come in." He shrugged. "I could use the overtime."

"Any word on the fire?"

"Not yet." He shuddered. "I hope they were already dead before it started." Then he smirked. "Cassano would've called them crispy, the sick bastard."

"Or marshmallows."

He'd had a depraved sense of humor. Turned out I missed that. Burke must have one too.

There was a somber silence for our lost brother as we entered the station. Burke forked toward the bunks. I went the opposite direction.

"Yo. Where you headed?"

"Been called to the principal's office."

"Ooooh." He slapped me on the back.

I flipped him the bird.

This was my first long shift since the suspension. Hopefully, that meant I was back full time. Captain didn't have much choice when we were a man down.

I tapped my knuckles on his partially open door.

"Come in." The call was gruff from too many years of cigarettes and whiskey.

He sat behind his desk with an unlit cigar hanging from his mouth as he studied an open folder.

"Hollingsworth, you're late."

He hadn't even looked at a clock. But I had before I turned off my truck. I was seven minutes early.

"You wanted to speak to me, sir." I wasn't in the mood for an argument.

"Don't sit. This won't take long."

I was halfway in one of the chairs in front of his desk. As commanded, I stood back straight.

"Who told you to work that fire last night?" His haggard gaze finally appraised me.

"Burke said it was all hands-on deck. Everybody close by was there."

"When did Burke become captain?"

I clamped my mouth closed. I was already on a razor-thin margin. Though the urge to defend myself pulsed underneath my surface. This time, I *hadn't* done anything wrong. Only what I was asked.

"You're out. Since Burke thinks he's in charge, he can bring you your stuff from your locker."

What?

"You need me on this shift. We're down at least a man—"

"You're done, Hollingsworth."

It was like he spoke a foreign language.

"I just got here. You could've told me on the phone you didn't want me in today." I thrust my finger in the direction of the bunks. "Those guys need me. I'm here. And I'm staying."

Captain crushed the end of his cigar in his fingers. Well, he wasn't the only one mad. This was absurd, even for him. And after the past few weeks, if he wanted to be the recipient of all my pent-up frustration, that was fine by me.

"I have work to do." I spun and stalked away from the man who'd had it in for me for as long as I could remember.

"Hollingsworth."

I hesitated in the doorway when he called my name but didn't turn around.

"You're fired."

CHAPTER FORTY-SIX

PEPPER

WHY DID *you tell him you were homeless?*

It wasn't his business. Only one other person on this earth knew. Did I think because we'd spent a few nights together and he was nice to me I could trust him?

But that look on his face when I'd told him the truth.

Shock. Then horror. Then pity. Then . . . I didn't know what the last one was, but it changed something between us.

Maybe it was a loss of respect.

I slammed the freezer door.

"Who wants ice?"

Was I trying to be falsely cheerful for the dogs or me? They could see through me, but I didn't want to project my bad mood onto them.

A piece of paper floated to the floor from the ferocity of the slam. It landed face up.

An old note of Vivian's ideas for the adoption event.

I stomped on it.

All the sweet faces I loved scampered toward me, eager for the ice. I tossed a piece to Sadie before she could bark.

As the sound of crunching grew louder as they all chomped away, I knew what I had to do.

These dogs were our family. I wanted them to be happy. I wanted them to have everything they needed.

And they did right here.

I slid down the cabinets to the floor. A free-for-all ensued with the ice.

My eyes stung.

Muffy licked the side of my face with his cold tongue.

"Do you want to go anywhere? To a new home?" My voice was watery.

He put a possessive paw on my leg.

I blinked hard to hold back the tears. The weight of everything pressed heavy on my shoulders.

Vivian's heart was in the right place. It was mine that was wrong.

My irritation wasn't at her or the adoption event. It was at myself.

I was embarrassed over this morning. I was angry we'd had to place some of our dogs in someone else's care.

I was scared Teague would disappear from our lives as quickly as he entered.

Sadie nudged the bowl out of my hands and crawled into my lap. She licked at my face.

I hugged her fiercely.

"I can't lose you," I said into her neck.

I found myself surrounded by all of them. They licked and sniffed and pawed at me in support.

Because they understood me better than anyone.

They were my safe place.

And lately our safe bubble felt penetrated.

This changes nothing.

Teague's final words from earlier pierced my brain.

"Think he's coming back?"

Ash pawed at me. She believed in him. Maybe I could take a lesson. Maybe I could stop being so guarded.

I checked the clock. After ten. Another day that had gotten away from me.

"We'd better tell Miss Adeline we're going for our night walks."

At her name, a few dogs bolted up the stairs before I was off the floor. The sound of their paws hopping on the hardwoods made me smile on a day I would've thought it impossible.

Dogs were the great healers.

I followed them to the base of the stairs and cupped my hands. "Hey, I'm running out to take a couple dogs out. I'll be back soon."

"Be careful. Take your phone," Miss Adeline called.

I pocketed the device and leashed up Sadie, Muffy, and Ash.

As the back door slammed behind us and we entered the dark alley, Teague's warnings about being out late at night popped into my head. I never thought about those things much before him. But I could be extra cautious. I always was.

Muffy did his business immediately like the good boy that he was. He looked at me for his treat. I fumbled in my pocket for one and finally found it.

He munched as Sadie pulled us toward the end of the alley instead of following Muffy's lead.

"You have no concept of cold, do you?"

She ignored me like always and headed in the direction of the park.

"Sadie, can we not go that way?"

The direction of the park still hurt too much. Seeing it earlier in the day . . . I needed some time away from it.

But she wanted to go that way, so we did.

There was no one else around. Who would be out in this cold? *Is it ever going to warm up?* A few cars passed every so often as we made our way down the block in the otherwise quiet night.

Sadie charged ahead until the park came into view. Where there used to be lights illuminating the perimeter, it was now a big dark hole.

Ash's steps were tentative the closer that we got. Sadie had been so sensitive to the other dog's feelings that I was surprised she barged forward.

Muffy was in between the two, unsure whether to speed up or

slow down. Ash's body was warm against my leg where she'd glued herself to my side.

Grrr.

Ash bared her teeth and refused to go any further. She hadn't had this reaction to the park earlier in the day. Sadie stopped. And sniffed. And barked.

Woof. Woof. Woof.

Muffy joined in but this wasn't his playful bark. It was deep and powerful and scary.

I glanced around but didn't see anything out of the ordinary. These dogs wouldn't be barking at nothing, especially not like this. Maybe it was anger somehow at the destruction of their park. It wasn't impossible for them to feel that even though they were dogs.

Part of me hoped it was Teague and he would appear from the shadows like the other night in the alley.

"Let's go home," I said. No need to stress them out any further.

"I think Garrison might've left some midnight snacks for you." Even the mention of a treat didn't stop the barking.

I tugged the leashes, unable to get them to move in the direction I wanted.

Maybe I need to go to an obedience school.

"Sadie." I hoped I could get her headed home and the others would follow.

I crouched down next to her and touched her head, but she kept barking. "What's going on?"

She lunged around me, knocking me to my rear. The leashes were yanked from my hand, the rope burning my palm.

Something went over my head and a sickly sweet smell invaded my nose.

I swung my arms wildly, hoping I didn't hit a dog but praying I'd nail whoever was around us.

A grunt sounded from behind me.

The barking was so loud I could barely hear my own thoughts. I tried to pull off whatever was over my head, but it tightened the harder I fought.

I have to get to the dogs.

"Run," I screamed, but it sounded warbled. Distant.

Please don't hurt them. Please don't hurt them.

And then I was in the air.

I landed on a hard surface that didn't feel like concrete. With everything I had, I kicked.

I struck something.

Pain radiated from my foot to my knee.

A door slammed.

The barks muffled.

And then everything went black.

ENJOY THIS BOOK?

You can make a huge difference.

Reviews encourage other readers to try out a book. They are critically important to getting your favorite books in the hands of new readers.

We'd appreciate your help in spreading the word. If you could take a quick moment to leave a review on your favorite book site, we would be forever grateful. It can be as short as you like. You can do that on your favorite book retailer, Goodreads, and BookBub.

Email us (grahame@grahameclaire.com) a link to your review so we can be sure to thank you. Together, we can ensure our friends aren't left out.

Thank you so very much.

ALSO BY GRAHAME CLAIRE

SHAKEN SERIES

Crash & Burn Duet

Crash

Burn

Rise & Fall Duet

Rise

Fall

Bend & Break Duet

Bend

Break

———

SHATTERED SERIES

Shattered Secrets

Shattered Sins

Shattered Lies

ABOUT THE AUTHOR

Grahame Claire is a *USA Today* bestselling author of contemporary romance.

A writer. A blogger. United by our love of stories and all things romance. There was definitely some insta-love. Hello? Books involved. A little courting. A lot of writing. The result . . . Grahame Claire.

Soulmates. Unashamed of our multiple book boyfriends. Especially the ones that rooted in our heads and wouldn't leave us alone. Don't worry. We'll share.

Pleased to meet you.

Our favorite thing about being an author is you, the reader. So please, reach out. If you want to get on the exclusive mailing list (trust us, you do), you can do that at www.grahameclaire.com/newsletter.

Let's chat books on Goodreads. We can gossip about our book boyfriends on Twitter at @grahamewrites, Facebook at www.facebook.com/grahamewrites, our Facebook group Grahame Claire Reader Hangout at www.facebook.com/groups/GrahameClaire-ReaderHangout, Instagram @grahameclaire, or send us an email anytime at grahame@grahameclaire.com.

Follow us on BookBub at www.bookbub.com/authors/grahame-claire

Printed in Great Britain
by Amazon

24415892R00148